HARRY FLATTERS

Carruthers J. Lardy

Grosvenor House
Publishing Limited

The right of Carruthers J. Lardy to be identified as the author of this
work has been asserted in accordance with Section 78
of the Copyright, Designs and Patents Act 1988

The book cover is copyright to Carruthers J. Lardy
Cover illustration by Neil Collins.
Circuit Maps by Neil Collins

This book is published by
Grosvenor House Publishing Ltd
Link House
140 The Broadway, Tolworth, Surrey, KT6 7HT.
www.grosvenorhousepublishing.co.uk

This book is a work of fiction. Any resemblance to
people or events, past or present, is purely coincidental.

A CIP record for this book
is available from the British Library

ISBN 978-1-80381-116-1
eBook ISBN 978-1-80381-144-4

Acknowledgements

The author would like to thank Bridget Bennett, Jim Prentice, Onky Levett-Scrivener and Miles and G Bennett for patiently reading the book as sections of it emerged, and Helen Aline Ball for knocking it into shape. Thanks also to Gladys Bunfield (Mrs) who helped with detailed proof reading and spotted a bad mistake before it was too late. Sincere thanks to Neil Collins for the cover illustration and the maps. Finally thanks to Tanis Eve in particular and all at Grosvenor House Publishing for their help and support.

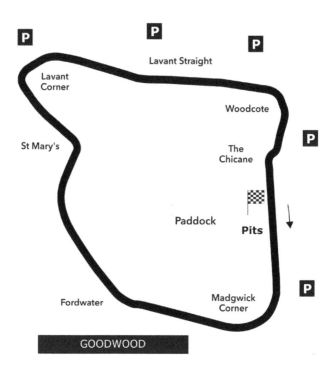

Burnenville

Malmedy

Masta Straight

Haut de la
Cote

Masta Kink

Kemmel

Les
Combes

Holowell Straight

Eau Rouge
Pits

Raidillon

Blanchimont

Start

Holowell

La Source

Clubhouse

Stavelot

La Carriere

SPA-FRANCORCHAMPS
1970

Les
Combes

Kemmel
Straight

Malmedy

Eau Rouge

Raidillon

Pouhon

Rivage

Blanchimont

Pits

Fagnes

Chicane

La Source

Curve Paul Frere

SPA-FRANCORCHAMPS
TODAY

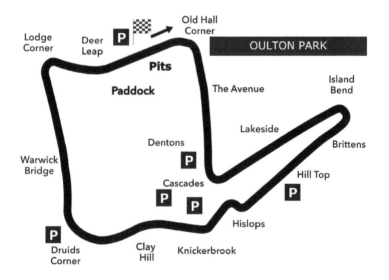

Lodge Corner

Deer Leap

Old Hall Corner

Pits

OULTON PARK

The Avenue

Island Bend

Paddock

Lakeside

Dentons

Brittens

Warwick Bridge

Cascades

Hill Top

Druids Corner

Clay Hill

Knickerbrook

Hislops

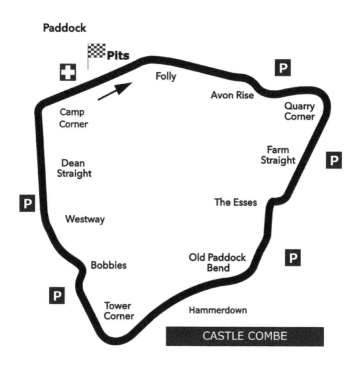

Paddock

Pits

Folly

Avon Rise

Quarry
Corner

Camp
Corner

Farm
Straight

Dean
Straight

The Esses

Westway

Old Paddock
Bend

Bobbies

Tower
Corner

Hammerdown

CASTLE COMBE

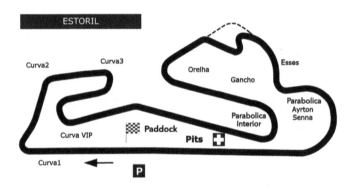

SNETTERTON

Montreal
Williams
Bentley Straight
Nelson
Oggies
Hamilton
Agostini
Brundle
Bomb Hole
Murrays
Paddock
Palmer
Pits
Coram
Riches

P P P P P

Harry Flatters was the term used
by racing drivers, particularly in the 1950s,
for taking a corner absolutely on the limit of adhesion.

1

I was enjoying one of the best days of my life when I saw Bill Akely die right in front of me. Pulling eight-two on the Lavant Straight at the Goodwood Revival in my pride and joy, a Ford Consul Cortina, developed by Lotus, known to the rest of us as a Mark 1 Lotus Cortina, I had just cleared the kink and had a few seconds' respite, giving me just enough time to look at the gauges: oil pressure OK, oil and water temperature OK. And we were in second place. I felt as much as heard Bill approaching from behind in his Ford Mustang. As he thundered past I glanced across at him. Both of us were wearing full-face fire-resistant balaclavas, but I could see from his eyes he was having as much fun as I was. He pulled in front of me ready to take the tricky double-apex right hander that is Woodcote corner. But instead of braking and changing down the gears he carried on at an undiminished speed. Even the scream of my engine couldn't mask the sound of him hitting the bank.

The trouble with someone going off in front of you is that your eye naturally follows what is going on, and it distracts you from the task in hand. Driving any sort of race car involves split-second timing, and the discipline to repeat the exercise lap after lap. You need to brake at the same point in terms of distance from the corner, and on the correct portion of track to line the car up for the bend.

Woodcote corner tightens as you go on. Professionals start from the middle of the road, miss the first apex and sweep into the second, kissing the inside and outside curbs in turn as they go. Done right it is enormously satisfying; it's one of the few corners anywhere where you don't use all the available road in order to maximise speed. Now I had a full-on emergency of my own. I was yards past my braking point, too far over to the left, and going too quickly. As I turned right the car yawed to the left underneath me, and headed for the wall just past the Woodcote grandstand. Out of the corner of my eye I saw a ball of orange flame engulf the Mustang. By now I was four feet onto the grass but hopelessly sideways, and I had run out of opposite steering lock. If I braked now the car would be a missile. My right foot was trying to force the throttle pedal through the bulkhead and the engine was screaming well past the recognised rev limit, all in the hope that the rear wheels would finally grip and I could get the car back onto the track. Just as I was starting to pick an impact point, they did.

The next problem was that I was not going to make the chicane; I was on the wrong line and going far too fast. There was nothing for it but to head through the gap to the left, normally reserved for the course car and the ambulance, with the car still twitching. Having shot through there at barely diminished speed, I eventually managed to slow down, and toured round to stop on the grid, having acknowledged the inevitable red flag.

As we all got out and removed our helmets and balaclavas, Max De Vries approached me. A white Bajan of great apparent wealth, he was descended from original plantation owners; he came over to Europe for the racing season most years, campaigning his Alfa Romeo GTA.

Yesterday his driving partner, Andy Steer, a British Touring Car Championship regular, had won the professionals' race in Max's Alfa. His brother Wilf, also a BTCC man, had come third in my car.

"Did you see what happened?" he asked.

"Yes," I replied. "It happened right in front of me. Is it bad?"

"The car was buried in the tyres and burning like hell, but the fire truck was already there," he said.

"That's easily the fastest part of the circuit," I replied, "he would have been going at…what, pushing 140 mph there? The impact will have been enormous. The odd thing is, though, he didn't seem to be trying to slow down. Or spin it to a stop."

We were joined by Reg Prescott – ardent enthusiast, saloon car racer for decades, and owner of one of the most original Mini Coopers out there. He had been well down the field, having been baulked at the start by a car that stalled in front of him.

"The fire was more or less out when I got there, but they didn't seem in any great rush to get Bill out of the car," Reg said.

A bad sign. I glanced up to my right and saw Bill's wife Claire and their two children standing on top of the pits, looking back down towards Woodcote. I didn't know Bill that well, having only been racing for two seasons, but he ran a Mustang restoration business with a stellar reputation; his cars always looked the best and went the best. Claire looked utterly alone. The giant screens were showing adverts back-to-back, which was also a bad sign. So, we waited, talked of inconsequential things, and worried.

Eventually the tannoy rasped into life and informed us that the rest of the St Mary's Trophy race would be cancelled, and that some time would pass before racing could resume again as the barrier needed extensive repairs. Mr Akely, we were told, had been taken to Chichester General Hospital.

We all got into our cars and drove back to our paddock berths. Almost as soon as I had parked the car, the tannoy started again. "Would the driver of car 67, James Westerfeld, please report to the clerk of the course?"

That would be me. An invitation like that wasn't optional, and it was usually the prelude to a bollocking at best and serious sanctions at worst. I walked through the crowds, still in my flame proof overalls, lining up in my mind my mitigation for cutting the chicane. The only thing in my favour was that I had known John Russell, the clerk of the course, for years – he'd run trips to the Nurburgring and Spa for enthusiastic amateurs.

I was ushered straight in.

"Hello John," I said. "Sorry about cutting the chicane – things were getting slightly out of hand at that point."

He half smiled. "That's not why you're here, James – although, that said, good save. You were right behind Bill Akely when he crashed, weren't you?"

Goodwood was covered in cameras; some were used for monitoring driving standards and some for the TV coverage. All of them fed into his office, so he knew the answer before I agreed.

"We've been told he's suffered a traumatic head injury, and they don't reckon he's likely to survive." He closed his eyes briefly. "You had the closest view of what happened. There'll be an enquiry at the end of racing today, and we'd like you to attend as a witness."

"Of course," I said. The logistics of this development ran through my mind. The original plan was to load up the car onto the trailer, bimble back to my parents' farm in Essex, drop off the car and trailer and then hot foot it back to London, hopefully not too late, to do some much-needed preparation for tomorrow's trial that I was due to prosecute. It was a simple enough drugs case, but one of my three opponents was Potter, a man I had been in pupillage with, and I loathed him with a vengeance. I had a long eight days in prospect. This weekend had been planned as an antidote to the stress of work. Then I remembered that Bill was probably dead, and felt like a prick.

"I take it that this enquiry may take some time," I said, pulling myself together. "It would help if I could leave my car on the trailer here in one of the hangars and fetch it next weekend."

"No problem." John looked back at me. "The aim is to convene here at 7pm after prize giving. It'll be me, you, the stewards, the Driving Standards Officer, and possibly the Duke of Richmond."

The Driving Standards Officer was usually a high profile retired professional racing driver who had the reputation and stature to keep the BTCC hooligans in line when they forgot that they were racing for fun and entertainment and started to punt each other off. In our cars. I hadn't met him before, but knew him by reputation.

"I'll be here," I replied. "Is anyone looking after Claire Akely?"

He groaned. "Didn't she go in the ambulance?"

"I last saw her on the roof of the pits watching her husband's car on fire. I don't know."

"OK," John sighed. "I'll find out and get someone to give her a lift if she's still here."

I walked slowly back to the paddock, wondering how a day that had started so well had gone so wrong. The previous evening had been the Goodwood Ball. This no-expense-spared extravaganza involved one of the hangars being decked out to resemble the decks of the Queen Mary. Upon arrival we were handed tiny bottles of chilled Veuve Clicquot and a straw through which to drink it. As we moved through to dinner, actors playing the part of well-wishers waved us off on our "journey". And just to top it off, the girl I had been sat next to had danced with me all night and then given me her phone number. She'd briefly wished me luck before the start, but I hadn't seen her since. Competitors weren't allowed to start packing up until after prize giving, so I contemplated going to watch the rest of the day's sport. But my heart wasn't in it.

When I got back to our bay, Terry, my mechanic, and Flora, the object of my attention last night, were both standing by the car.

"Are you OK?" they asked in unison.

"I'm fine," I replied. "I was right behind Bill though when he went off. I made the schoolboy error of watching what he was doing and not what I was doing, so I missed my braking point and nearly had the mother of all accidents trying to sort it out. I've over-revved it for sure."

"I'll check the clearances and see if the pistons have hit the valves," said Terry. "And a compression test. These days Lotus engines are surprisingly robust."

Really? That had never been their reputation in period.

I explained that it would be next weekend before I could get it back to his workshop. He nodded, grunted and started packing up the tools he had brought with him.

I explained to Flora that my plans had changed as a result of the stewards' meeting, and that while I would be going straight back to London, it would be later than I had hoped.

"Don't worry," she replied, "I'm going back with Susan." If I remembered correctly, Susan was her flatmate.

"Can I call you in the week?"

She laughed, and turned away smiling. Some good news then.

The rest of the afternoon was spent in the drivers' suite watching the racing on the TV screens. The atmosphere was subdued. After the prize-giving I returned to John Russell's lair. I was the last one there – the Duke, three stewards from the organising club I didn't know, and Tim Jackson, the Driving Standards Officer, were all gathered around the table.

I asked if there was news of Bill, but there wasn't any. We got straight to it.

I explained that I had got past the kink on the Lavant Straight, had seen Bill approach me to my right, slip past, and glance across. So far, so normal.

"I followed him for a few seconds, with the gap widening between us, as you would expect. And then he just carried on. No brake lights. No sign of the nose dipping. No attempt to spin it. He just went straight in."

"Are you certain he didn't brake?" John asked.

Before I could answer the phone sitting on the table rang. John answered.

"Hello. Yes. Yes. I see. Thank you for letting us know. Goodbye."

He looked around the room. "That was the hospital. I'm afraid Mr Akely died ten minutes ago, which means the police and an inquest. James, you're a barrister – what happens from here?"

I explained that the Coroner and his officer, usually a serving policeman, would lead the enquiry from here. "By all means conduct your own enquires, though the MSA will. You don't need me to tell you that it's probably better to dovetail in with the authorities."

"Right," John said. "We'll be in touch."

The Duke just sat there, looking stricken. He had created this wonderful event from scratch. It had run successfully for over twenty years. We all knew though that it was running under a number of safety waivers, and this accident had the capacity to kill the event off. He had resisted the suggestion that debris fencing was necessary, hoping to keep a period look to the circuit. But the reasons that had caused his grandfather to stop racing here at the end of 1966 had not gone away: primarily the lack of distance between the edge of the track and the point of impact, aggravated by the high ambient speed of the cars. No-one was entirely sure how he'd persuaded the safety authorities to allow him to hold the event.

When Bill had hit the bank some of the tyres forming the protective barrier had escaped their tethers and had gone into the five-deep crowd. They, quite understandably, had recoiled from the situation, causing some crush injuries as people fell over. Others were burned in the ensuing fire. Five people were in hospital, condition unknown. More were in the medical centre at the circuit.

"There's a military term for all this," said the Duke softly. "Fucking disaster."

After that, there was nothing else to say. I returned to the now deserted paddock, put my car on the trailer, parked it where I had been told I should, and set off back to London.

2

The journey back had been miserable. An accident on the A3 slowed the usual Sunday night traffic, increased by Revival attenders, visible due to the predominance of tweed and furs crewing classic cars. Some of them had overheated in the jams and sat looking smart if disconsolate on the roadside, waiting for recovery. I finally fought my way back to Hammersmith at 10.45pm, then I sat down to tackle the jury bundles and final polishing of my case opening. I'd got into bed at 2.30am, but hadn't settled. All I could see was Bill's car thumping the barrier and bursting into flames. So, I was not in the best of shape when the alarms went off. I had two of them, the legacy of sleeping through one when I was a pupil and being late for court.

I arrived at Kingston upon Thames Crown Court to find the robing room heaving. It's a twelve-court centre and a number of multi-handed long trials were in progress; if you added in cases like mine that were due to start, and all the backing trials – there as cover in case they didn't – space was tight.

Despite all the preparation, including disclosure requests having been made weeks or months before, there was always a final sort-out on the morning of trial; this in turn meant giving the officer in the case the list of disclosure requests and praying for a quick turnaround. Mercifully, for once, the list was short.

I looked at the list for court 9. There were three cases – in theory, all short – ahead of us. I wandered down to the Crown Prosecution Service room, and bid a cheery hello to the team who worked there. Cheerful, invariably understaffed and thus hopelessly overworked, they made prosecuting just about bearable.

"Anyone covering court 9?"

Cath Brown put her hand up, but she was on the telephone trying to find a missing witness in another case, and I knew that in any event she would be covering at least two other courts. Eventually she got off the phone and I checked that she'd received the email detailing the jury bundles.

From there I walked round to the police room to touch base with the officer in the case, known to all in the trade as the OIC. He was present and told me that the first and only witness due that day was already there and busy reading his witness statement. So, in theory, we were good to go.

I told him the list of outstanding requests and was greeted with the familiar response – "I gave that to the CPS months ago." It was a standing joke. Defence makes disclosure request to the CPS. The CPS pass it on to the OIC. The OIC responds with the requisite information, which is then never seen again. This nonsense could be repeated two or three times before the issue was sorted out. It was easy to blame the CPS for their inefficiency but it wasn't really their fault; cuts had decimated the number of staff they could afford and had weeded out many of the good ones. I'd lost count of the number of drinks invitations I had received over the last few years announcing that so-and-so was leaving/retiring/going to pastures new, and would I like to join them in some distant bar in, say, Tolworth, to say goodbye? Those who were foolish enough to remain could only fire-fight. I wandered back upstairs to the robing room with my head full of what I was going to say to the jury about all this.

Not much, as it turned out, because defendant number one was in custody. It seemed that it had slipped Wandsworth Prison's collective mind that they had him, and had not put him on the van with the other prisoners. Panicked steps were now being taken to get him here, which in my experience meant we had a solid few hours of faffing before he actually arrived.

We finally got into court at just before noon. We explained the position to the judge – a good sort, whom I'd known for years – and so we waited. By the time the defendant arrived, well after lunch, all we had time for was swearing in the jury and a short summary of the case from me. Instead of a full-ish court day, we had achieved almost nothing. On the upside, I was out of there by 3.30pm.

-

The week ground on. The case proceeded in bursts with numerous interruptions and late starts. By Thursday morning though, I had closed my case. Now it was their turn. The facts were straightforward. The police had performed a stop on an ageing Ford Focus at 2.30 in the morning, having been tipped off by our witness that what appeared to be drug dealing was going on at the end of his road. Inside they found the three defendants, £895 in cash in the centre console, and two kilos of high-grade cocaine in a holdall in the boot. During their interviews all three had denied knowledge of the cash or the drugs. The fingerprints of the front seat passenger were found on some of the wrappings, and the mobile phone found on the guy sitting in the back proved to have pages of texts and emails which were strongly indicative of him being a dealer. No such material linked the driver to the drugs, but he was the driver, it was his car, and he was forty miles from his home in the middle of the night in the company of two men he professed not to know. One way or another, they had a spot of explaining to do.

Our witness had been heavily challenged, but he had stuck to his guns well, helped, I rather thought, by being courtesy itself. This was particularly true with Potter, who had tried to rile him into a reaction, with it having evidently slipped his mind that the jury were listening to this. As he got ruder the witness had got more polite, taking time to consider his answers and not reacting when he was interrupted every time he stopped to draw breath. Eventually the judge had admonished Potter at some length in front of the jury, which I had definitely not enjoyed at all.

The first defendant was the rear seat passenger, whose mobile phone records smoked a bit. He spent an hour denying everything and was then asked some inconsequential questions like, "What brand of cigarettes do you smoke?", by counsel for the two co-defendants. After lunch I went to town on his phone records, assisted by the fact that he couldn't disown the phone because it contained a number of enthusiastically sexual messages from his girlfriend. I never look at the jury until delivering a final speech, but my sense was that at one point they, or at least some of them, were laughing at him.

When I got home that night I found a letter from Sussex Police informing me that they were investigating the death of William Akely and they had reason to believe that I could help them with their enquiries. Could I please contact the email address provided so that the investigating officer could speak to me?

Less expected was what was waiting on my answering machine. A female voice, clearly close to tears, informed me that it was Claire Akely, saying that she hoped that I did not mind her calling me, that the Goodwood authorities had given her my home number, and that she badly wanted to speak to me. Could I ring her back?

I called the number she had given, heart pounding. I was nervous, partly because whatever I said would be wholly inadequate for what she was now facing and partly because I had said little more than "hello" to her before. The phone rang twice before she answered; clearly, she had been waiting for the call.

"Hello Claire. James Westerfeld here, returning your call. I'm so sorry…"

She interrupted me before I could finish the sentence. "Thank you. Thank you. I'm so grateful to you for calling me back. I…" She broke down sobbing.

I waited. What could I possibly say?

After a minute or so, she audibly got a grip and started again. "I'm so sorry. It's been…I don't know where to start. The clerk of the course – John something? – gave me your number – he told me that you were right behind Bill when he crashed."

"Yes," I said, "he came past me about half way down the Lavant Straight. We glanced across at each other, and I could see he was smiling. It all looked under control."

"Please, tell me what happened. Why did he crash? He was a good driver. He wouldn't make a mistake like that – " There was another pause, and I could hear her trying not to sob again. "I need to talk to you, but I don't want to do it over the phone. There are things. Things that weren't right. Or not normal." She hesitated. "It's possible… it may not have been an accident. I just – I don't know."

Ah.

"Where do you live?"

"West Norfolk. I could come to you, or meet you half way. But please, I have to meet with you."

She was clearly desperate, so I thought through my schedule. Tomorrow: all day in court and a few pints in the evening with a fellow petrolhead who lived round the corner. Early start Saturday to go and rescue the car, with a view to getting it back to Terry's by the time he closed.

"I can meet you on Sunday, if that's convenient?"

In the end I agreed to go to her home. It was easy for me, and she would have to park the children with someone if she came to me. Not really the week to leave them. She gave me directions and we agreed that I would be there at 10.30am.

I'd barely hung up when Flora rang.

"Hello, James – how's your week been?"

"Quite hard work, but we're getting through it. Last weekend has been on my mind quite a bit, and Claire Akely rang me today."

"Bloody hell," Flora said. "What did she want?"

"I'm not sure. She seems to think that there's something wrong, and wants to talk to me about it – it's probably nothing." I shook my head, trying to set it aside. "Now, much more importantly – might I persuade you to come out to play?"

She giggled. "I don't frequent the playground much these days, but seeing as you asked so nicely…I can do next Tuesday, if you like. What about The Roebuck? It's about half way between the two of us, and the food is good – say, 8 o'clock?"

"Done! I look forward to it. What are you up to this weekend?"

"I've been invited to a party on a friend of a friend's yacht, which is currently moored in Southampton – apparently it's usually in Antibes or Antigua, so best behaviour I'm thinking."

"Very smart. Do remember us peasants when you get back."

She laughed and rang off.

3

I was up early on Saturday, keen to get the car back to London by early afternoon. It was entered in the Spa Six Hours race, which was scheduled for next weekend – that meant leaving with the car, kit and co-driver on Wednesday. Genius though he was, there was no way Terry could strip and rebuild a Lotus twin-cam in two working days; if that was what was required, we would have to scratch. It had sounded all right when I switched it off, despite the abuse I'd given it, but I was no engineer.

I slid into the driving seat of my beloved Senator. Now 25 years old, it was, to me at least, the perfect saloon car. Designed as General Motors' response to the then current BMWs and the like, it had fantastic handling and sounded great on semi-open exhausts. Mine was an unbelievably rare 5 speed manual. It was still quick (enough) and its rather anonymous looks suited me fine, as I tended to travel at what could politely be called a reasonable clip. It was also a fantastic tow car. Its huge boot swallowed anything we needed in the tools department, and it was stable with the Cortina sitting on the trailer on the back.

When I had started to follow historic racing in the early 1980s, I had just acquired my first car, a glacially slow 1960 850cc Mini. It leaked for England in the rain, but it was transport; I took myself off to numerous race meetings across the country, usually organised by the Vintage Sports

Car Club. In those days everyone, no matter how glamorous or valuable their kit, transported their cars either on an open trailer, towed usually by a Ford Granada estate or a Rover SD1, or converted Duple coaches. If you were really pushing the boat out you could get a shrink-to-fit Lycra condom for the car, which kept the rain off it even if it didn't disguise the shape. Things had moved on a bit since. Although historic motor racing was strictly amateur – in the sense that the most generous prize would be a set of tyre vouchers, or at Goodwood, a cigar – it had become more professional in the way it was done. Hired professional drivers were often in the fastest cars, and ex Formula One transporters carried them. Arriving at Spa in a Senator with an open trailer would put us in a minority of about one.

I made good time and was at the circuit in under two hours. I had been a bit worried that there would be no one about, but there were a number of bodies dismantling the grandstands and the various booths used over the Revival weekend. The hangar containing my car was open, and I lost no time in hitching up. Also in there, much to my surprise, was the wreck of Bill's Mustang. As no one was watching, I wandered over to take a look.

The front was telescoped into the footwell and the A post was crumpled. The fire damage was slight. As the driver's door was half open, I looked inside. The steering wheel was bent, and one of the seatbelt mountings had sheered off, which was definitely not supposed to happen. That might explain the head injury. It had all the hallmarks of a car that had been in a heavy accident, but nothing that looked dramatically out of place. I would need to get underneath to see if, for example, the brake lines had been cut.

Get a hold of yourself! I thought. *Cut brake lines – are you mad? People don't get murdered at Goodwood. They get murdered outside chicken shops in Peckham at two in the morning, and you know that because you prosecute the idiots who stab them. Pull yourself together, man.*

Taking the most trailer-friendly route added about half an hour to the trip, but I was still in west London by lunchtime. Terry's workshop was in a yard hidden in darkest Kilburn. The first time I had tried to find it I had done so with written directions, and even then it had taken two more phone calls to hit the target. Today the gods were kind, traffic was light and the yard, shared with three other businesses, was clear. Once there I put the ramps down, started the car without difficulty and reversed into his workshop.

There were strict rules at Terry's. First, all matters required consideration over a mug of tea. No exceptions. Second, there was a pecking order as to where you could sit in his office. A glorified booth, there was just enough room for his desk, usually covered in a mountain of paper, alongside an immense ashtray, a filing cabinet, and three chairs set back against the walls. As usual, Terence already had a cup of tea and a roll-up on the go. He was on the phone while studying a chess board, one of the cheap fold-out ones you can buy from any charity shop for 75p and that look like they've been chewed by someone's Dobermann at some point. The first time I'd been to Terry's I'd assumed the chess board belonged to one of his kids, although I'd later learn that his boys were all grown petrolheads by that point. I'd made a light comment to that effect and Terry had grinned at me.

"You're a barrister, right?"

"That's right."

"So, you're pretty clever? Good at strategy an' that?"

"So my clients tell me – at least, the ones who aren't in prison."

Terry's smile widened. "I've been learning how to play chess," he said. "Slowly, like. My wife loves it. I reckon a smartarse barrister like you ought to trounce me, but I'd be interested to see. Fancy a match?"

This hadn't been what I was expecting, but Terry had come so highly recommended that I would have danced on the table if he'd asked me to. Besides, I *was* a barrister, and I *was* pretty good at strategy, and I reckoned if I beat him cleverly, he'd respect me more. My brains were all I had to work with.

So I sat down across the table from him and watched as he slowly lined up all the pieces; I politely offered to let him be white, which made him smile again.

Within six moves, I was beaten. I looked up from the chessboard, unable to believe it.

"God, that was lucky, eh?" Terry said. "Come on, let's try again – no way I'll ever be that lucky twice."

So we played again. This time, he got me in five moves.

"Terry," I said, as I surrendered my pieces for the second time. "When you say you've been learning how to play chess – how long have you been learning?"

Terry grinned, showing off the gap between two of his teeth on the left side. "My wife's a grandmaster," he said, "so I've been learning off her since a little before we got married."

"And when was that?"

Terry's grin got even wider. "Twenty-five years ago, give or take."

I burst out laughing. Terry clapped me on the shoulder appreciatively, and we've never had a problem since.

Terry raced V8 engined stock cars and nothing consumed his attention like a conversation about racing. From what he was saying at my end, this might take some time. One son, his brother and the brother's son were all in the same series – the Evans family could make up half the field. And just because they were family did not mean that they went easy on each other. More than once I had seen one or other of them limping or with an arm in a sling as a result of a particularly muscular on-track manoeuvre.

Terry knew where to find the best parts. For instance, in period, a Lotus crankshaft was made of cast iron, which ensured that it couldn't safely be revved higher than about 6000rpm. Now, with modern metals, 8750rpm was possible. I had been at the top end of that sort of zone when I was trying to get off the grass at Woodcote. It had to be said though, that along with the upgrade in performance came an upgrade in price. The crankshaft and con rods alone had cost just over £15,000, so I was keen to keep them if possible. The options I faced were:

a)   completely got away with it;
b)   a valve had made light contact with a piston which would need a cylinder head rebuild only; or
c)   a total strip down and start again. Parts and labour, to you, Sir, £20,000. Plus VAT. Now, would you like a cup of tea?

While I was ruefully mulling over that he appeared to notice that I had arrived. We started to chat about the events of the previous weekend. As an entrant I had tickets and passes to spare, and I had offered him some. He had been keen, but the lack of affordable hotels within a fifty-mile radius of Goodwood nearly put him off, before he'd discovered a cousin with a caravan down the road. As we hadn't really talked while at the circuit, I'd already explained over the phone earlier in the week the details of what had happened and now relived it again. It was clear that as a stock car racer who spent almost the entire lap sideways, he felt that I had rather over-estimated the peril in which I found myself. We got to it.

He rolled a snout and got to his feet. "Compression test," he mumbled, and went in search of the relevant kit.

The compression tester was a gauge that looked like a tyre pressure gauge with a flexible metal tube coming off the bottom of it which had a threaded end which, in turn, screwed into the spark plug hole. He disconnected the coil, removed all four spark plugs and ordered me into the driving seat with instruction to press the starter. As the engine turned over the gauge measured the compression in that cylinder. In a perfect world they would all be the same and all over 150 psi.

After repeating this exercise four times he paused.

"Looks like you've fucking got away with that. 160 to 165 on each one."

Then he really surprised me. He produced a device that looked like the sort of thing doctors insert up your bum and put it down each spark plug hole. In it, apparently, was a small light and a camera, and with me turning the engine over by hand he could see the tops of the pistons and the state of the valves as the engine rotated.

"You're a jammy fucker. No rebuild required."

Phew! I arranged to leave the trailer there, asked him to change the oil, put the tallest differential in it and check and adjust the brakes. With that I pointed the Senator in the direction of Hammersmith, feeling that I had dodged a bullet.

At home I called Michael. Michael Ferguson was my co-driver at Spa. We had met twenty years previously on one of the Nürburgring trips that John Russell helped organise.

Just about old enough to be my father, we'd got on from the start, made each other laugh like children and, perhaps most importantly, as drivers were about the same standard. Both of us had wanted to race as young men. For different reasons we'd not done that, and both rather regretted it. Both of us took it up when we were far too old to become professionals and both thought that driving a classic car at a historic race meeting was one of the best ways of spending a weekend. When we'd met he'd had a Triumph TR3A and I had a TR4. He had upgraded to a fully race prepared E Type Jaguar, but then an expensive divorce had intervened, so was without toys for a bit. At the time I was racing a Riley 1.5 so we'd shared that for a couple of years. Since then I had co-driven his Volvo Amazon and a Works Austin Healey Le Mans Sprite. He was particularly pleased with my latest acquisition, the Lotus Cortina, bought with a legacy from an aunt I had never met.

As a proud Scotsman, Michael was in total thrall to Jim Clark, and fancied three wheeling it around Spa. We had both been there before and loved the atmosphere, but our efforts to coordinate a test day had come to nothing, so he had yet to drive the car. As it was, I had only driven the car at Brands Hatch, Oulton Park and Goodwood, so was a bit apprehensive. The speeds achievable at Spa were way faster than the norm, hence the need to raise the gearing by changing the diff. As we were now definitely going, the plan was for him to get the train to London on Tuesday and let himself into my place with his key. He would have to amuse himself; I was planning to be otherwise engaged with Flora.

4

Sunday dawned overcast, with drizzle apparently to follow. I wasn't sure how long it was going to take to get to the Akely's, so pointed the Senator north at 8.15am. Traffic in north London was light and I was on the A1 heading towards Baldock in 40 minutes. My destination was a farmhouse near a village called West Dereham.

Claire opened the front door as I got out of the car. Two dogs, a Labrador and a Jack Russell, flung themselves out, keen to sniff the interloper. Behind Claire in the doorway I could see her children peering past her. She shouted at the dogs, and welcomed me in.

"This is Eleanor, and this is Jake," Claire said, turning to them. "Mr Westerfeld has come to talk about daddy."

"I'm sorry about your dad," I said to them. They nodded, but neither said anything. Claire despatched them to the snug to watch videos, and I was ushered into a large farmhouse kitchen, the sort of room that is part cooking venue, part dining room and part sitting room.

"Thank you so much for coming all this way – I've been beside myself with worry. How are we going to carry on? I can't run the business, I don't know anything about cars…I'm so sorry, I forgot my manners. Do you want tea or coffee?"

And then she burst into tears.

I moved around the island and handed her my handkerchief. "Look," I said, "I'll help you if I can. I'm not sure what you think my qualifications to help you actually are, but I'll do my best, alright?"

She nodded.

"Start at the beginning."

They had met, it seemed, at Snetterton circuit. She had zero interest in cars, but had an on-off boyfriend who was racing a Ford Falcon who had persuaded her to drive up from London to watch him race. It was raining, she was cold and wet, and they had had a row within an hour. Bill had taken pity on her, asked her into the awning attached to his van and offered her a cup of tomato soup. They only stopped talking long enough for Bill to win his race. She had watched him coming through Russell corner, in the rain, neatly sideways but still under control, and had for the first time understood what the point of this might be.

After the race, over more soup, he had explained that he was renting some sheds off a friend of his father's, that he wanted to get into the race car preparation business and that the car was his shop window. Within weeks they were together, and she spent more time in his tiny rented flat in Downham Market than her own in Clapham. After six months of spending every weekend in Norfolk and getting the early train back to London on Monday mornings, she had given up her job at an upmarket estate agents in Brook Green and moved to Norfolk for good, parental disapproval ("He doesn't even have a degree!") notwithstanding.

And she'd been right. The business had prospered due to his engineering nous, helped by being a bloody good driver in all conditions, which made the cars seem fast and reliable. He wielded the spanners; she kept the books. After four years the farm buildings had come up for rent, and despite the sums seeming enormous they had gone for it.

As the business grew they acquired more staff – at the current count four mechanics and an elderly chap in his late seventies who notionally swept the floor and made the tea. Life was good. The children came along, and there was enough cash coming in to pay the mortgage. Better, Bill's reputation spread internationally, and he was preparing cars for a number of wealthy clients. Two in particular: Timo Aristophanes, whose family seemed to own most of Greece, and Max De Vries, the Bajan Alfa driver.

This caught my attention. "Why did Bill prepare his car? It's not American, doesn't have a V8 engine. It isn't his area, surely?"

"Bill had worked on my father's Alfa when it broke down one weekend in the early days. It was part of what broke the ice between them. He figured that one engine was much like another, and as long as you knew where to get the bits it was OK. Max appeared in the paddock at a race somewhere and asked Bill to look after his car. We needed the work, so…"

"But it sounds like the business is in good shape," I said.

"It was," Claire said. "But we needed better trucks. Bill's first lorry was so old that it had originally seen service with the Coal Board. He made it like new, but it was slow and couldn't carry more than one car plus the tools. He upgraded as we went along – but the international work meant trucks that could go all over Europe. Now we have two trucks, and own almost nothing." The enormity of it all hit her again and she crumpled slightly. I had seen the trucks. Shiny and enormous. Car transporter one-minute, capacious living room the next.

"OK. Setting all that aside for a moment – look, when you called, you seemed to think something was wrong."

"I'm not sure I *think* something was wrong," Claire said. "It's more of a vague feeling. I kept the books, always had. But something changed. Bill and Max had a huge row here one weekend, about three months ago. Bill wouldn't say what it was about. Up until then he had told me everything."

"Did Bill have any medical conditions?" I asked.

"He had very mild asthma which meant he had to have a test once a year for his race licence. And he had mild glaucoma diagnosed in his right eye about a year ago. He got eye drops for that. He was a fit man."

"How much work have you got on at the moment? Can you keep going in the short term? Can one of the men step up to help you with running it all?

"I have thought about that," she replied. "Tolly, the old man, ran his own workshop for decades. He's a friend of Bill's dad. We more or less created the job for him because he was bored at home, his wife had just died and he wanted something to fill in the day. When they're away on race trips, Bill said that he comes into his own and runs the pits brilliantly."

"Would the others mind the promotion?" I asked.

"I don't think so," she replied. "They're all young. Two have young families. They're terrified that they'll be out of a job before they've found new ones."

"Right. Here is what I suggest you do," I said. "Call Tolly today and warn him about him being in charge. Then when the others get here tomorrow morning, have a staff meeting and tell them that their jobs and pay are guaranteed for the next three months, come what may."

"Three months?" She gripped the edge of the table. "I can't think past tomorrow."

"You don't have to," I said. "You need to project confidence, confidence that you may not feel. There are two main threats to your livelihood: customers taking the work away, and the men leaving when there's still work to do. How loyal were they to Bill?"

"Three of them were solid, I think. I'm not too sure about Michael."

"If he goes, will you cope?" I asked.

"Yes."

"So, tell them that they're guaranteed work for the next three months. Ask them to pledge that they will stay for the three months. That buys you time to try and see where you're going. You'll have a much clearer picture of everything then. Have you heard from the coroner about Bill?"

The post mortem was inconclusive. There would be another in the week. She didn't know when the body would be released back to the family, or, as a result, when they might be able to hold the funeral. Before I left I asked to see the accounts. Claire took me to a small study from which she ran the business.

"Can I borrow your accounts and the books? I'll try and see if there are any irregularities or anomalies," I said.

"You're so kind," she said. "I can't think what I would have done if you hadn't been here."

"Are you here alone with the children?" I asked.

"Yes. Bill's parents called by, but they're in a worse state than me."

I could imagine.

"Get a friend to come and stay. You'll feel better for having someone else here."

I loaded up the car with ledgers, books of accounts and the cash records, and bid her farewell. As I drove away I caught a last glimpse of her in the rear-view mirror; pale, beautiful, and utterly alone.

5

We'd wrapped up the case by 10.00am on Tuesday, and within three quarters of an hour the jury went off to consider their verdicts. Cases running to the wire were a fact of life at the Criminal Bar, and plenty of us had missed holidays, or at least the start of holidays, because cases had overrun. You only needed a couple of sick jurors to play havoc with the scheduling. The key to it was getting your speech in, then you could, with the client's and judge's permission, scarper. Today, it was to be hoped, we would actually get a result. I would be free.

The jury had been out for just over an hour and a half when the tannoy went: all parties in Khan and others to court 9. Could be a question, could be a verdict. I gathered my computer, notebook and sentencing guidelines and took the lift to the top floor.

Three guilty verdicts later, I was heading home.

-

Michael arrived as I was walking out the door. These days he lived in the south of Scotland, but when married he had lived in Wiltshire and the ex-wife and three children divided their time between there and London. He used my place as a *pied a terre* – I was usually around, but he could come and go as he wished. I told him that I didn't think I'd be late, and we agreed to chat over a nightcap later on. Feeling good about life I walked towards Chiswick, relishing the much-needed exercise. The aim was always to try to get there before the date.

As I walked, I wondered, somewhat idly, about how I had managed to get to my late thirties without getting hitched. There had been a few near misses, including one girl who had moved in for eighteen months. She had then moved out again, and I had not been that bothered; enough said. Flora Bascombe was unexpected. She was the sister of a chap I had vaguely heard of who raced in historic Formula Junior; we'd hit if off immediately, and I had much cause to praise my good fortune as we danced until chucking out time. She worked in business relocation for a company in Gunnersbury, lived with a mate, knew her own mind, and seemed to have life well sorted out. The fact that I thought she was stunning didn't hurt either.

We arrived at exactly the same time. As the conversation flowed, I learned a bit more about her. Her parents were now divorced. Her father was a minor aristocrat with a roving eye. Her mother, long remarried, lived happily in Devon, and there was also a house in Italy. As we talked it dawned on me that she worked because she wanted to, not because she needed to, and viewed life as an amusing game. She was thirty, she said. How had she not been snapped up? Answer: long relationship with a motorcycle enthusiast which ended with him dead through no fault of his own. She had two brothers, both bankers of one sort or another.

It would not have been lost on her that blowing what cash there was on a racing habit I could barely afford was not wholly conducive to frequent trips to Porto Fino, and I was beginning to suspect I was a touch out of my league. But when I leaned in to kiss her cheek at the end of the evening, she smiled up at me with unmistakable affection. I walked home slowly, grinning. The world was at my feet.

-

I had something of a fitful night, mainly because of the childish excitement I still got from going motor racing. We were up, breakfasted, and ready to go by 8.00am. I loaded helmets and holdalls into the car, together with every spanner I owned; Michael was a good engineer, and his input would be welcome should there be trouble with the car.

Amateur motorsport needed a surprising amount of kit. Though in no other way could you compare either me or Michael with Lewis Hamilton, we had to wear the same equipment. Motor racing safety was treated very seriously these days, partly because of the gladiatorial toll exacted upon drivers up to and into the 1980s. So we were both padded to the gills: flame proof shoes, flame proof socks, flame proof pants, a flame proof roll neck long sleeved T-shirt, three-layer flame proof overalls, flame proof gloves and a flame proof balaclava helmet, topped off with a full faced crash helmet. Even if all this kit was in immaculate order it was all lifed and had to be changed every three years. It was as hot to wear as it was expensive to replace, and every item was checked for condition and date at scrutineering. What with that, regular clothing and tools, the boot was nearly full.

We crept through the morning rush hour to Kilburn where Terry's brother was waiting for us at the garage. Terence, it seemed, was not keen on anything so rude as an early start. He knew that I would call in and pay him when we got back, and in any event had yet to prepare the bill. We loaded up the car, checked that we had spare wheels, put the fuel jerry cans back into the tow car and tied it down. Once hitched and with the electrics connected, we were ready.

We fought our way out of London, survived the M25, and drove at regulation speed down to Dover and the ferry. Once embarked we enjoyed a very cardiac unfriendly all-day breakfast and a snooze. The plan was to take it in turns to drive through France and into Belgium more or less as far as Liege, and then turn south. About an hour later we would be approaching the town which had given its name to healing waters everywhere: Spa. We made good time, so were at our hotel in time for dinner and some healing Belgian beer. We retired to bed before we really started talking bollocks.

-

Official scrutineering and practice did not start until Friday, but that didn't prevent us making a prompt appearance in the paddock in order to get a decent spot, offload the car and generally take in the lay of the land. There were no fixed rules, but people in the same series tended to stick together, so the Cortina was not about to find itself amongst the 1950s Grand Prix cars. There was to be a drivers' briefing in the main pits/grandstand at 3pm, which left a number of hours to kill.

Nothing if not amateur historians, we decided to look around the old circuit. With the emphasis on safety these days, which usually manifested itself in slowing down the cars, it bore remembering that there was a time when circuits devoted their attention to speeding them *up*. Spa and, in particular, Reims, had a running battle to see who could run the fastest grand prix. Both were on closed public roads. Reims held its last F1 race in 1966, but Spa has continued to host a round of the World Championship, albeit on a track in truncated form. It was still partly public road into the 1990s.

If you start at the hairpin bend at La Source, the road runs down a surprisingly steep hill towards one of the most iconic corners in the world. Having passed the old pits, still used for sports car racing, and with your transport reaching terminal velocity, you hit Eau Rouge. It's actually three corners, not one. First there's a flat left flick – I say "flat", but unless you are carrying some serious aerodynamic downforce you will have had to brake because of the Radaillon. This is an uphill right hander so steep that while you are actually negotiating the corner, all you can see through the windscreen is the sky. If you're on the wrong line on the way in, there's a stout wall on the right-hand side to catch you out at the top. Assuming that you haven't run out of real estate as the car goes light and the road starts to level out, the road bends to the left again. More potential here to clout the wall. Then you are faced with a climbing straight to Les Combes. Here the new circuit spears off to the right, but the old track carried straight on over a crest and started to run downhill. At the bottom was a never-ending right hander called Burneville. By now you are in the countryside, and then as now the main occupation here was farming cows, which then as now were fenced in with barbed wire. The young but supremely talented Chris Bristow got it wrong at Burneville in the 1960 Grand Prix, going through a fence and being decapitated.

Just to keep it interesting there is the odd farm building in the firing line on the outside of the track. After Burneville comes a short straight, then Malmedy corner. Simple enough in itself, the real aspect of note was that the speed through Malmedy factored your speed down the Masta Straight. The Masta Straight is *loooong*. And in the middle, just when you are wondering if your engine, which has run at peak revs for over thirty seconds, will go bang, comes the Masta Kink.

In 1950 Luigi Fagioli, piloting an Alfa Romeo 158, was timed going through here at 200mph. Left-right between houses. Michael and I got out of the car to see if we could establish how he did it. Other than sampling the excellent frites served in the target on the left as you exit the corner, we had no idea.

There are perhaps three sections of road which once hosted Grand Prix that can be described as genuinely terrifying: the Fuchsröhre at the Nurburgring, the downhill sweepers after the pits at Rouen, and this one.

The road then carries on straight down to a climbing uphill well-cambered right hander, known as Stavelot, after which it straightens. You're now heading, flat-out once again, towards the other great modern racing challenge: Blanchimont. The new track filters in from the right; there's a left-hand kink and then a short blast to a sharp left hander, which you are supposed to take flat, aero or no aero. Suffice to say that it requires big *cojones* to do so, and the consequences of arriving at the wrong speed on the wrong line are likely to be both expensive and painful. Having navigated that, you are faced with the "bus stop" chicane to slow the F1 cars down before entry to the modern pits. And so down to La Source to start the whole adventure again.

We spent a cheery hour and a half reminding ourselves why the GP boys in the 1950s and 1960s were short on imagination and long on courage. When we got back to the paddock we parked the car and Michael went off to find a coffee. Along the row where the Lotus Cortina was parked I was astonished to see a Bill Akely liveried truck.

They had laid things out as smartly as the lorry: neat tape marking off their empire, some deckchairs and the sides of the trailer expanded out, denoting that it was now in living room mode. As I hovered near the tape a short, trim, grey-haired man, looking for all the world like a retired major in his sixties in a tweed jacket, striped tie, and neatly trimmed moustache, emerged from the bowels of the hospitality unit and asked if he could help me.

"I'm James Westerfeld," I said. "Claire Akely asked me to help her after Bill's death. I must say, I'm rather surprised to see you here."

"Anatoly Romanoff," he replied. "We are running Timo Aristophanes' GT40 in the Six Hours, and Max De Vries in the one-hour touring car race."

"So you're Tolly?"

"Certainly am," he grinned, "Claire mentioned that she'd asked you for help, so if there's anything we can do to assist you, you only have to ask."

"We have a drivers' briefing in forty minutes, but maybe a quick coffee?"

"Come on in." He beckoned me into the entertainment suite and busied himself with the coffee machine. "We felt that we should come to this meeting. Claire was very insistent that we continue to fly the Akely flag." I smiled. "It feels like the fun has gone out of it without Bill, though. He was such an enthusiast. How do you take it?"

"Black no sugar, thanks. Who have you got here?"

"Me and two mechanics. Bit of a skeleton crew. We had to leave two men at home to get the cars ready for Oulton Park next weekend. We've never run the team with just the three of us."

"Well, if you need help, Michael and I are also in the Six Hours. If we fix it so that our cars are in the same pit, whichever one isn't in the car can help you."

"Very kind of you, old man," he replied. "What are you running? If there are only two of you, we can hardly impose."

"Lotus Cortina – we're just here for the craic."

"Fine car, that, though," Tolly said.

I took a sip of my coffee; and then I couldn't contain my curiosity any longer. "Look – Claire said that something had gone wrong. Something that she couldn't put her finger on. She said that Bill and Max had had a stellar row, and Bill wouldn't tell her what it had been about. Did you know about that?"

He paused for a moment, then nodded. "I did. I wasn't there for the argument, but one of the boys heard some of it and said that the two of them were shouting – and I mean *really* shouting – at each other. He thought they'd start fighting. In the event Max left, apparently mid-sentence."

"Where did this happen?" I asked.

"Back at base."

"Claire told me that you more or less ran the team when you were away racing . Did you see or hear anything out of the ordinary?"

He laughed. "I'm just the gofer – Bill was very much in charge. He did seem a bit tense about two months ago, but I didn't pay too much attention to it at the time. It was about that time though, that we were coming back from a meeting at Zolder, and when we got to Dover, Customs gave us the third degree. They took the truck to bits, totally dismantled it – it took us more or less the whole night to rebuild it so that we could get home. Normally they just wave us through – we travel abroad often enough to start to recognise some of the staff at the port." He paused again. "Didn't find anything, mind, but a major embuggerance. Do you think that might have had something to do with Bill's death?"

"I don't know," I said. "Probably not, but…well. If you think of anything."

"Of course."

We finished our coffees and got up to go out. "Where are your cars?" I asked.

"You obviously haven't been to Spa before. Rule one: get to the paddock early, offload the cars and bag a garage. We're in garage 12. If you're lucky there may be room for a small one with us."

He headed off in the direction of the sports car pit garages, and I walked back to our car.

The drivers' briefing took far longer than usual, mainly because it was conducted in three languages: Dutch, French and English. It was mostly the normal guff: if you crash here it's going to hurt since you'll be going so quickly, obey the flags, don't exit the pit lane unless you're shown a green light, the entrance to the sports car pit lane would be via the GP pits, and generally: behave.

After it was finished Michael and I wandered over to garage 12 to see if there was any space. The only person there was wearing Bill Akely Motor Sport liveried overalls; I told him who we were and why we were there, and it was clear that Tolly had been as good as his word. There was a Cortina sized hole alongside the left-hand wall. This was a complete bonus; normally the touring cars were seen as the poor relations, entrant in the Six Hours or not, and had to stay outside.

With practice tomorrow morning at 11 o'clock there was not much more to do. All the detail jobs such as oil change and brake checks had been done by Terry, so we left the car, piled into the Senator and pottered back to the hotel. There we reminded ourselves why Belgian beer in general and Trappist in particular is such dangerous stuff. Dinner was enjoyed on a shared table with a Northern Irishman whose accent was so thick that half his funny stories were barely penetrable. It did not stop us laughing until we cried.

-

First practice demonstrated once again what a cosmopolitan world historic racing is. The field numbered over one hundred cars. At the front were those of the serious players like Timo Aristophanes, who was fielding his ex-works Le Mans Ford GT 40 in full Gulf livery. As well as being a very special historic car, it was well prepared and well driven, something Timo did not leave to chance by dint of hiring as his co-driver, Wilhelm Groen, who was a current DTM hotshot. There were about four other serious contenders for victory in GT40s.

Then down a notch, came things like E Type Jaguars and 2 litre Chevron sports racers. A well driven E Type was theoretically capable of winning the race, but it usually required trouble to strike the front runners. Also, at this level came Ford Mustangs and Falcons which, although notionally "street" cars, in fact pumped out getting on for double the power they had once had and had suspension set-ups of a design that would have mystified their manufacturer. They made up in power what they lost in height and weight.

Then you got to the mid field such as us with the Lotus Cortina's and Alfa GTAs, as well as some MGBs, Triumph TRs and Austin Healey's. And at the back, presumably spending much of the lap peering into the rear-view mirror watching for quicker machinery, was a father and son team in a Ford Anglia. Chances of victory: zero. Amount of fun to be had: unquantifiable.

Before going out to race I always got very nervous. I found much of driving unconscious, in the sense that if, say, the car snapped sideways without warning, I was able to apply opposite lock before my conscious mind had registered that we had a problem, which sounds fantastic, but added to the nerves, precisely because my conscious mind was not in charge. What would happen if my brain let me down?

The nerves manifested themselves in constant yawning, which I couldn't fathom until I read an article about the late David Purley. He was an ex-paratrooper, and as such had had to jump at night. He made up in sheer courage what he lacked in driving talent when driving in Formula One, and faced with heading into the downhill swerves at Rouen without lifting, the crest into this section being inconveniently opposite the pits so all could hear the bubble-footers, he would shout into his helmet to ensure he kept his foot in. During his time in the army, waiting to jump, he described getting the yawns from fear. And the penny had dropped. Yawning is a by-product of adrenalin, and adrenalin is important. There's a fine line between being sufficiently revved up on adrenalin and mental paralysis. Get it right and it had the remarkable effect of slowing things down to manageable proportions. Not enough adrenalin and sooner or later you would make a mistake. Or drive like a wanker.

I sat strapped into the car, wearing all the kit, and idly noticed that it was shaping up to be a scorcher. That said, you never quite knew where you were with the weather at Spa. It could be budgie-smugglers and sun cream one minute and a torrential downpour the next. Two legendarily talented British drivers, Dick Seaman and Archie Scott-Brown, had died here, nineteen years apart, at the same corner, simply by arriving at a soaking wet corner at dry speeds. That didn't look too likely at the moment as we sat and roasted, facing down the hill towards Eau Rouge in the pit lane, waiting for the green light, but you never knew.

Because we'd found a garage space, I was rather nearer the front of the queue than I had wanted to be, so for the first couple of laps of this session I would be peering into the mirror, trying to stay out of the way. The plan was for me to do five laps, check if everything was working OK, set a time, and then send Michael out. He was competitive enough to want to beat me, so at least we would, between us, do the car justice.

The light went green. The car was already warmed up so it started immediately and we went down the hill in first gear. At the bottom I opened it up, keeping to the right side of the road, and on cue two GT40s and a Mustang thundered past as if I was tied to a post. We had set the mirrors up with some care, as pulling into the path of a much faster car to take a corner was not recommended, however much you were entitled to be there. At the top of the hill I moved left into a conveniently empty track and swung right into the new section.

At Les Combes you are faced with a sharpish right-left, immediately followed by a right named Malmedy; then you go down a hill towards Rivage. This is an odd corner. Essentially a very wide right-handed hairpin, you turn almost completely back on yourself while still going downhill. Piling on speed though is not an option, as the camber is so adverse that as the car leans to the left it feels as if it might fall off the hill.

After this there is a short straight leading into an unnamed left hander, and then you start going downhill fast. Even the Cortina accelerated like a piano falling out of a window here, and waiting to greet us at the bottom of the hill was the left-hander, Pouhon.

Purists claim that most of the true driving challenges have been taken away from Formula One, and with the modern I-will-build-you-a-racetrack-in-your-car-park approach, they are largely right. But not here. The track goes downhill all through the corner, which is in fact two corners albeit taken as one. Being too brave too soon is the path to idiocy, so I dabbed the brakes, slotted third and turned in. If you are going fast enough, and if you have the line right, the car will start to drift. Get it right and the steering unwinds as the car, by now at an attitude of, say, thirty degrees to the corner, starts to wash towards the outside of the track.

No drift on this lap, but we touched the outside kerb at the correct place and then moved back to the next apex which has now presented itself on the left-hand side. Kiss that and, now back into top, heading straight towards Les Fagnes. This is a right-left combination, still all the while going downhill, which in turn leads to a quick-ish right hander named Stavelot.

Almost immediately after this is the Curve Paul Frere, named after one of Belgium's most distinguished drivers. Taken nearly flat, it's a right hander which as you exit it re-joins the old circuit which has fed in from the left. Speed through here determines how fast you go down one of the properly quick sections in world motor racing.

By now you are on the valley floor and approaching top speed, which, with tall gearing for us, would be about 135mph (no one carries speedos in race cars; they just add weight); now we come upon Blanchimont. Faster than it looks, it's a real sorter of cars and drivers, and a well organised combination will make up time here that was lost getting up the hills. Negotiate that OK and you are almost immediately hard onto the brakes for the Bus Stop. Straight on for the pits, left for the run down to La Source, and then down the hill to Eau Rouge.

By now, happy that the tyres were warm, the brakes were good and the temperatures and pressures were as per, I opened it up down the hill. Two quicks passed me as I went past our pits, and a third was far enough back to allow me to take the ideal line into Eau Rouge without spoiling it for both of us. At the top I kept right to let the traffic by and concentrated on playing myself in and getting the lines right.

I had two reasonably clear laps before I brought it back to the pits. Pouhon had at least been taken in top gear, although there was more speed to come. I hopped out, Michael hopped in, and I helped him do up the belts. There too we were similar in height and build, so no elaborate measures were required to accommodate both Jack Spratt and Humpty Dumpty. The door shut, and Michael was off. I could hear the hollow sound of the Lotus Twin Cam as he shot up the hill.

I took my helmet and balaclava off, and unzipped the top of the overalls, and settled down to wait. A good time round here for us was in the region of just over three minutes.

Tolly wandered over. "You were going well," he said.

"Thanks," I said, "it seems to be running OK, although it's bloody hot in there – it'll be very uncomfortable tomorrow."

He laughed. "At least we have the engine behind the driver."

Heat was one of the reasons why driver fitness, or lack of it, was an unseen hazard. To those watching, you're sitting down and the car is doing all the work, so what's the problem? What they don't see is that you are wearing enough to keep a moose warm; what with the G forces and bracing with your legs across the car to keep upright in the seat, it was a surprisingly aerobic experience. Weight loss guaranteed, particularly in a saloon car designed before in-car ventilation was much of a priority, compounded by the heat-soak coming back from the engine. Even the gear lever could get too hot to touch. If you couldn't take the heat either you'd pass out in the car or your stint would be measured in minutes. The strict annual medicals weren't for show.

"How are you boys getting on?" I asked.

"Timo has been out and in, and Wilhelm's now in the car, so we'll find out what a quick time is."

He had been kind enough to place our pit signal bag, containing board, signal numbers and letters, and clipboard with stopwatches against the pit wall. I readied myself to time Michael as he came past on the first flying lap. Right on cue he flashed past, the car sounding crisp. He did four further laps and then came in. He had shaded my time by just under a second: 3 minutes 7.08 seconds.

No drama: further practice tomorrow, when I would have a proper go. The main thing was the engine was in good shape after the Goodwood excitement. Once it had cooled off we checked the brakes, and on the principle that if it isn't broken, don't fix it, we left it alone. In Formula One it was remarkable how the reliability of the cars improved after they banned the team mechanics from fiddling with them after qualifying.

At that point Tolly appeared with the provisional qualifying times: Aristophanes GT40 on pole and the Westerfeld/Ferguson Cortina 55th, with a couple of Ford Mustangs behind us. Not bad! We placed the sheet under a windscreen wiper and resisted the temptation to mark our names with a highlighter pen.

I introduced Michael to Tolly and we were promptly invited into the Akely truck for coffee. Michael asked him how a man with such a Russian name found himself in England.

"It was my grandparents," he said, "they had a number of estates across Russia. Come the Revolution they had to leave in a hurry with almost nothing. My grandmother managed to bring her jewellery, which helped set them up when they got to England in 1920. There was quite a well-established white Russian community here, and eventually my grandfather got a job as a farm manager in Norfolk. With that came a house, and so my father and aunt were brought up there; eventually I grew up there too. About the only Russian thing about my upbringing was the name. Although I was Anatoly at home, the kids at school called me Tolly and it stuck."

"What did you do?" asked Michael.

"I had my own workshop. General repairs to cars and lorries. It was the sort of village garage that many places had, with a small shop and some fuel pumps at the front. I enjoyed it, and it was a good living. But eventually we weren't selling enough petrol or diesel to interest the fuel companies, and they stopped selling to us. I could see which way it was going and managed to sell it to an optimist who thought he could make it pay. I was retired for fifteen years. Then my wife became ill and died."

"I'm so sorry," said Michael.

"It's OK," Tolly said. "I've got used to it, and Bill was kind enough to give me something to do. It wasn't the money – it was the boredom after she went that I struggled with. And I love going racing."

"Do you think you can keep the business going?" I asked.

"In the short term, yes. I'm seventy-eight, but I'm fit and I still have most of my marbles. I can run it day to day. But

Bill was the strategic thinker. He knew where he wanted it to go and was good at attracting work. Without him we'll survive for a while, but eventually the customers will go elsewhere. What a mess."

I tried to change the subject. "Did you have any trouble coming to Spa? You mentioned Customs had been a pain last time."

"No," he replied. "Straight through. We'll have to see what happens on Monday on the way home though."

We talked a bit more about this and that, and then Michael and I decided to watch the practice of the other races from different points around the circuit. We changed back into our civvies and hopped into the Senator. With a bit of exploring and a bit of intuition, we were able to watch the cars spitting out of the top of Eau Rouge, which in the case of the front-engined single seaters was properly exciting. I noted that Wilhelm Groen was aboard a 250F Maserati and giving a couple of Coopers – much more recent machinery – a hard time. We bickered happily about whether it was easy to drive such a beautiful car, or whether the brilliant driver was *making* it look easy. We would never know: neither of us could afford to buy or race a 250F.

As if on cue there was a roll of thunder. I looked out of the driver's window to see that while we hadn't been paying attention to the weather, dark clouds had moved in overhead, and that it was about to pour with rain.

In theory this would make no difference to the cars out there, as they pre-dated slicks by about twelve years, so would not need to change their tyres. When it started though, it was clearly a shower of biblical proportions, and car control was almost impossible, not helped by the fact that the track had been bathed in hot sunshine for days, and was therefore greasy. I watched a Ferrari 500 pop over the top of the hill going backwards, followed by a Maserati spinning out of control and saw the red flag. Just for a moment, the image of Bill's car bursting into flames played again in my mind; and then the moment passed, and Michael and I went to get some lunch.

6

On Saturday we were due out at 10am, this time for a total session of an hour and a half. It was cooler, the forecast was dry, and we hoped to improve on yesterday's times. We took our time getting changed, and joined the throng about fifteen minutes after the green flag. Long though the lap is, with the field numbering over one hundred cars, traffic remained an issue.

Michael went out first and did nine laps, bettering yesterday's time by four tenths. I took it easy for the first lap then turned up the wick. I had a clear run down the hill to Eau Rouge and managed to get it turned into the Radaillon going faster than I had before. As I braked to turn into the right hander at the top, I noticed that I was carrying 500 RPM more than yesterday. I kept it tidy through Rivage and down the hill, held my breath, and turned left into Pouhon. Immediately the car yawed right, but with opposite lock and the power on it came back to me, and we drifted through the whole corner with the car in an attitude, the steering wheel in the straight-ahead position. The perfect 1950s four-wheel drift.

I kissed the kerb on the outside, tucked it back into the second apex and barrelled into Les Fagnes, now 600 RPM up on the day before. Just Blanchimont to go; I drifted through, got it stopped in time for the Bus Stop and was clean at La Source. I blasted down past the pits feeling pleased with myself, pretty sure I had beaten Michael and certain that I had done as much as I was capable of. I did four more laps and then came in, having not been so lucky with the traffic again. I pulled up outside garage 12, switched off and undid the belts.

"Well?" I said.

"Bastard," said Michael. "3.02.98. You beat me."

"Well, it is my car, so I should! I've done as well as I think we're going to – I suggest we save the car for tomorrow. What handling changes do you suggest?"

"It's pretty predictable. It rolls a bit more than I would like, but I realise that we can't have just a dry set-up – we have to be ready for rain. Leave it. Do the fluids and the brakes and leave it."

"I agree. Goes all right, don't you think?" I replied.

"Yes," he said. "I never got the feeling though, that it was going to cock a front wheel like they did in the 1960s."

"It won't. The spring settings are completely different these days. And in any event, you'll have more grip if you've actually got all four wheels on the ground."

"Fair," he said. "Alright, you take it round to the paddock and I'll wait for you in the garage."

I climbed aboard, made a pretence at doing up the belts, explained to the marshal at the pit exit that I was actually going into the paddock and drove round to garage 12. We donned overalls, topped up the oil which had gone down a bit, reset the rear brakes, and when it had cooled down sufficiently, checked the water. No movement. Good. We then watched the rest of our group from the top of the pits, watching who was quick, who was wild and who was slow.

Back at the garage, Tolly had put a time sheet under a windscreen wiper: 47th overall!

-

Sunday was hot. Blisteringly so. The in-car temperatures would be murderous. Suddenly I envied the open sports cars, having spent yesterday pitying them in the rain. We faffed, pretended to be busy, and fretted. The race this year would start at 4pm and run until 10pm. That meant that the last hour and a half would be run in the dark. I had had fancy hi-beam lights fitted which lit things nicely, but I was more worried about being blinded from behind by a quick car, or not being able to judge closing speed and distance in the mirror because all you were looking at was a blinding splash of light. It was the first night race for both of us, although Michael professed not to be bothered. Or maybe he just hid his nerves better.

Having checked, rechecked and checked the car again, we watched time slow to a crawl. This was the bit I hated the most. Eventually, finally, at 3.15 we were summoned to the holding pen. Because of the number of cars in the field, what that meant in reality was a monster queue, snaking round almost all the paddock. It took the organisers about forty minutes to get everyone into qualifying order and the race off to a rolling start. We had decided that Michael would start on the basis that he felt more confident in the heavy traffic during the first few laps. From there it would be one-hour stints, governed in part by fuel consumption.

Because of the enhanced risk of an accident or fire, those of us watching were not allowed to stand on the pit wall for the first ten minutes. By the time Tolly and I took up our station it was clear who was leading – Timo's GT40 – and a whole lot less clear where we were. It took a further five laps before Michael acknowledged with a thumbs up my place on the pit wall. From there I gave him the lap times and, when they came through on the track data sheet, our position. He was doing 3.06 to 3.07 steadily, and as the field spread out we got into a rhythm. When it was my turn we were 51st. He refuelled on the way round and handed over to me a healthy if stunningly hot car.

As I launched myself in I wondered if I would cope with the heat, but by the time I had got to the top of the hill at Les Combes, I had forgotten all about it. Ahead by about fifty yards was an Alfa GTA – very much a direct competitor – so I used him as a yardstick of how we were getting on. As the laps ticked down, I slowly reeled him in. I was more or less right behind him, hacking down past Michael and Tolly in the pits, when a glance in the mirror revealed two Lotus Elans and an AC Cobra, nose to tail in that order. I kept right and let them get by, as did the Alfa. As they cleared the Radaillon, the extra power of the Cobra told and he breezed past. He did not, however, get clean away and as I was braking to turn into Les Combes the three of them were still in sight, nose to tail once again going down towards Rivage.

My plan was to stick behind the Alfa until the run down to Pouhon and hopefully pass him down the hill, but if necessary dive up the inside on the way in. I managed to get alongside as we approached the corner, aware that I couldn't use all the road, so dabbed the brakes and turned in, and promptly saw what appeared to be a plane crash.

Chunks of fibreglass littered the road. The second Elan, missing its nose, was in the wall on the outside of the circuit. The Cobra was upside down and on fire. What really got my attention was the remains of the first Elan, barrel-rolling along the top of the outer retaining wall against the debris fencing, shedding bits of bodywork, with the top of the cockpit appearing to take the bulk of the impact.

The marshalling at Spa is good, and there are two posts at this point, but it was instantly clear that with three seriously damaged cars they were going to struggle to cope. Because

I'd not been going as quickly as I would have been had the track been empty, I was able to slow down through the corner and pull off on the outside of the road just past where the first Elan had come to rest. The driver wasn't moving.

I undid my belts and climbed out, not looking forward to what I was going to find. Out of the corner of my eye I could see three marshals running back towards us from Les Fagnes. The car was smoking. I pulled my handheld extinguisher from the Cortina and ran over.

The Lotus Elan 26R is a lightweight racing version of an already light and minimalist car. To go racing one had to fit a roll cage, with a view to protecting the occupant in scenarios like this. Bouncing down the wall with the top of the cage taking repeated impacts had had the effect of pushing it into the cockpit and onto the driver. His helmet was visibly dished and blood was slowly soaking his overalls from a cut somewhere in the neck area. The whole car stank of fuel.

I had once been on a first aid course, but I was not a paramedic. Do I pull him out and make his injuries worse, or wait for the professionals?

The decision was made for me when, with a deceptively gentle "whoomf", the front of the car caught fire. I ran around and aimed my extinguisher at the base of the flames; while it had some effect, it didn't put them out.

Nothing for it then. I went to open the driver's door, which came away in my hand, undid the seatbelt buckle, and started to pull him sideways out of the car. At that point the marshals arrived. Two took over with the extraction, and a third tackled the blaze.

The exact infrastructure at Spa was beyond me, but there must have been cameras covering this section of track, because the next thing to hove into view was a fire truck, closely followed by an ambulance. The marshals motioned to me to leave, so I walked back to my car. By now I could see red flags out, so I motored slowly round to the rear of the queue of cars which stretched back to before the bus stop chicane. There drivers were standing by their cars, helmets off, so I joined them.

My mobile phone buzzed in my pocket: Michael.

"Are you OK?" he asked.

"Yes. There's been a big one at Pouhon, right in front of me. A three-car pile-up. I had to get out and help. It's nearly the end of my stint – can you take over? I'll get it refuelled and bring it round."

"Is it bad?" he asked.

"Very. The chap I dealt with is unconscious and bleeding, and the car was unrecognisable."

"What was he in?"

"An Elan 26R."

"Oh, shit. Nothing between him and the accident, then. Will they stop the race?"

I shook my head. "I doubt it. There are three cars to recover and possibly two more drivers to scoop up, but I think we'll be running again in twenty minutes."

He rang off. As I had guessed, almost immediately we were issued instructions to put our gear back on and return to our cars. I cruised round to the fuel station, topped it up, signed the chit, and stopped next to Michael.

We swapped quickly and off he went. As a result of the hiatus, the field was thoroughly bunched up, and it took half his stint for them to spread themselves evenly around the track. My stopping to help had cost us nearly thirty places. Tough luck: there was no handicapping system in this sort of racing, even for good Samaritans. Nevertheless, he worked his way back up the order, so when it was my turn to take over, we were lying in 60th.

By now the interior of the car was, if possible, even hotter. I played myself in again over the next few laps, noting with interest that as I went up the Radaillon, the view of the sky now included dark clouds. Both the car and I could do with cooling down. Michael and I had calculated that we would get away with not having to change the brake pads and shoes over the course of the race. How much they were actually worn was unclear without stopping for an inspection, but the pedal was long and getting longer, which meant either no meat on the pads or the heat from the brakes themselves was close to boiling the brake fluid. A wet track would reduce the wear on both brakes and tyres.

Rain, though, brings its own problems, starting with visibility: simply put, there is none. The spray from the cars ahead creates a low, impenetrable cloud, and that's before whatever arrangements for demisting the windscreen are taken into account. Picking braking points becomes guesswork.

On the upside, a wet track is a great leveller, as plenty of decent amateur drivers appeared to have had the morning off when racing in the rain came up at school. In our domestic UK series the Mini Cooper exponents did rain-dances on an hourly basis, because it moved their cars up from midfield to the front.

Despite the fact that I got even more nervous if rain was a prospect, I went well in it. As long as I had some idea where I was on the track and could see enough to be safe, a climb up the order was in prospect. All I had to do was gauge which bit was wet and which was still dry.

We didn't have long to wait. As ever at Spa, it wasn't the sort of light shower beloved by BBC weathermen; it was closer to the sort of industrial dowsing that Noah would have recognised. It came in from the south, which meant that the valley floor got wet first before the whole circuit was sodden. I throttled back, and watched with amusement drivers who ought to have known better clattering the barriers. Disappointingly, that then meant the Safety Car being deployed, so no overtaking.

I was only half way through my stint, so it made no sense to come in. We toured round, cooling car and driver, and I noted with satisfaction that the brake pedal started to behave normally again. After about fifteen minutes of this, the Safety Car went in and we were racing.

This time I went for it, and passed bigger, faster cars more or less at will. The car remained predictable in its handling, but the transition to oversteer took place much faster. The spray was manageable, the screen clear, and I was having a ball. Far too soon, the "IN" board was shown. With some reluctance I pitted via the fuel dock.

"The brakes have come back," I shouted at Michael as I hopped out. "It's slippery but consistent everywhere. Enjoy!"

Times were twenty seconds a lap slower, and it was getting dark as he went out, but he passed fifteen cars during the first twenty minutes. We were now an amazing 27th.

By the time it was completely dark, spotting Michael relied as much on the stop watch as it did our eyesight. He was still turning in sub 3.09s and still climbing up the order. When he came in for the final time we were actually on the leader board. He shouted that it was drying, and that the big V8s were starting to pass us, then helped me into the belts.

I drove down the hill into my first night race. My biggest fear, not being able to judge the speed and distance of faster cars approaching from behind, was more perceived than real. Occasionally I was blinded by something, but I worked out that the brightest lights, unsurprisingly, usually belonged to the fastest cars, so I did not have to spend too much time lingering out of the way.

That said, as the track dried, all our good work passing the big cars was being undone, as they made up for lack of grip or lack of enthusiasm when it was wet. I was soon into a rhythm and passing the odd car. I was delighted to see the Anglia still plugging round, and hoped that they had had a clean race. With mechanical breakdowns in these long races, if you remained reliable you could do well, even if brick-slow. There was every chance that they would not finish last.

I kept it tidy, drifting through Pouhon and Blanchimont, and generally felt that God was in his Heaven and all was right with the world. When the chequered flag came out, though, I was pleased to see it, as we were finally out of brakes and the tyres were not far behind. Our calculations had proved correct; and best of all, the car had not missed a beat.

As we were nowhere near the podium, I joined the line of cars filtering into the paddock and switched off outside our garage. Michael appeared in civvies, armed with two beers and a bottle of water. Rehydrating on beer is fun but unwise. Rehydrating on Trappist is suicide.

After the podium ceremony Tolly invited us back to the transporter, where we met Timo Aristophanes, Wilhelm Groen, and the two mechanics, one of whom had brought his wife. Michael and I had taken the precaution of laying in a supply of beer which was added to the Akely stash, so an increasingly noisy party ensued. We had finished 29th out of 70 survivors, with no other Lotus Cortina's or Alfa's ahead of us. The Anglia had managed 67th.

As our hotel was in Francorchamps we walked – or rather weaved – back there in the early hours. Amazingly the owner was still up, and had laid on cold meats and sandwiches for us. We wolfed them down, resisted the temptation to drink yet more lethal Belgian beer, and retired, knackered and happy.

That happiness barely lasted six hours. As we stumbled downstairs for breakfast, the race organisers' website – into which we were all plugged for essential communications – put out a press briefing announcing that Jeremy Smith, nineteen-year-old son of well-known historic racer Dougal Smith, had died in hospital overnight. He had been driving his father's Lotus Elan 26R when it was involved in an accident at Pouhon with two other cars during the Spa Six Hours race. Despite quick and efficient work by the marshals, he had sustained severe head injuries in the impact, and had succumbed overnight. The organisers sent messages of sympathy to his family. The other two drivers involved in the collision had minor injuries and had been discharged from the Medical Centre.

Two fatalities in two consecutive weekends of racing was unheard of. I struggled to think of when the last driver racing historic cars had even been seriously hurt, never mind killed. The racing community was not so small that everyone knew everyone else, but if you were around for long enough, you got to know who people were; so while I couldn't recall ever speaking to Dougal Smith, I knew who he was and would recognise him.

Breakfast was pretty silent. Michael had asked me what I had seen over beers the night before, and now I thought about it again. I had inferred, without dwelling on it, that two cars had tripped over each other, and that they were travelling so close together that all three became involved. At high speeds, and particularly once airborne, cars would behave unpredictably. If, for example, the Smith Elan and the Cobra had been side by side and the wheels interlocked, with both cars wearing eared spinners, the forces involved were more than enough to launch a car into the scenery; particularly if it was light, like the Lotus. But I was guessing.

It was a subdued journey back to England.

7

Mrs Gladys Tomlinson was the pensioner from central casting. She had an open, smiley face, a cloud of hair that would have been white if she had not rinsed it blue, and was everybody's friend. I was rather banking on her coming across well, because she was due to start her trial tomorrow at Inner London Crown Court for benefit fraud.

The Prosecution case was that when her husband had died some fourteen years before, it had slipped her mind to mention his passing to the authorities and had continued to draw two pensions, until a chance visit from the Department of Work and Pensions had established the truth in the autumn of last year.

We might have had more luck had she been in a position to repay the money, which totalled just over £138,000.

"Oh, I couldn't do that, dear," she had said to me, smiling, "I've spent it all! After Reg died, I started going on cruises."

And so she had. Two or three times a year, on the QE2 before it was decommissioned, and then on anything else that floated. She was so well known to them that she was given Frequent Sailor Points.

Mrs Tomlinson appeared to think that being prosecuted in the Crown Court was a minor inconvenience, with no downside. While most sensible judges would bend over backwards not to lock up a little old lady, on the figures alone she was staring straight down the barrel of two and a half years. An early guilty plea would help a lot, but Gladys wasn't having any of that either.

"Well, I don't think I've done anything wrong, dear," she had said when we broached the subject. Even when I gently pointed out the potential consequences, she just beamed and said that she wanted a trial.

The downside of this, aside from the fact that I was now going to have to think of some halfway plausible defence strategy for the world's most good-natured benefit fraudster, was that I now had a free afternoon. Usually this was the opposite of a problem, but since Jeremy Smith's death I'd been unsettled, the accident ticking through my mind over and over. It occurred to me that this would be a good moment to look over Bill Akely's accounts.

I started with the cash books. Written in neat copperplate handwriting, they were a record of the petty cash: money for milk or teabags. I turned to the invoice records, and found that regular customers received regular bills. Cross-analysis with the receipt's ledger showed that Bill's clientele paid on the nose, usually by bank transfer. Nothing looked out of place.

I thought it might speed things up if I concentrated on the period of the big argument and the search by Customs. Nothing stood out immediately. It was only when I looked at the bank statements that a couple of anomalies became apparent. On two occasions that I could see, there had been payments into the company account with no associated paperwork in the form of an invoice. The sums were not in themselves huge, but they weren't pocket change either. Both had come from bank transfers, and the account numbers of the paying bank were different. Both, however, had come from the Bank of Cayman.

I rang Claire Akely's home number, and she picked up almost immediately. I told her how pleased I had been to see the Akely flag still flying, and what a star I thought Tolly was.

She laughed. "He's already made suggestions for the future of the business. Mad really; I know nothing about cars, and he won't be around for ever. I've spoken to all our customers, and they've all said that they'll stay in the short term. The men have all said that they'll stay for at least three months too. But I'm going to have to make some decisions at some point."

"You'll get there," I said. "Just one step at a time. Listen, I have a quick question. I've found two payments from the Bank of Cayman for which there are no invoices. Do you know what they're for?"

She paused. "No, I don't. The Bank of Cayman? I suppose – but it's strange I didn't spot that."

"I only did because I was actually looking for something out of place. I take it Bill didn't mention them?"

"No, he didn't. When was this?"

"Both payments were in June this year. I had wondered if the big row might be significant, although I can't see how."

"The only link we have with the Caribbean is Max De Vries – but he used to pay us with a UK bank account, from memory," she said.

"I know," I said. "I've matched his payments with his invoices, and the paying bank for them was Barclays. OK, leave it with me. When do you need all the ledgers back?"

"Whenever is convenient for you – I'll reimburse you if you post them."

"Don't worry, I won't post them. It might help me to have a look round the workshop and see the set-up."

"Why will that help?" she asked.

"There's no real reason why – I just thought that if I absorbed some of the atmosphere it might help me think like Bill."

The following morning I got to Inner London Crown Court early. Gladys, though, was earlier. I found her sitting outside Court 1, in a matching two-piece suit, hand bag on her knees and sporting a hat that looked like a squashed fruit pastille. "Morning dear," she trilled.

"Good morning Mrs Tomlinson," I said.

"Please call me Gladys, everybody does," she said.

We had been through this before. I took her into one of the few conference rooms, and in what I hoped was the nicest way, went through again what to say and what not to say in court. No first names, call the Judge "Your Honour", not "dear", try and look at least a bit crestfallen, listen to the question, give short answers, and don't fence with my opponent.

"No dear," she said. I could see that I was wasting my time, and it dawned on me rather later than it should have done, that, notwithstanding the clear and present risk to her liberty, she was having the time of her life.

We had drawn HHJ Kaur, a smart, tough, female judge who was now the Resident Judge, which meant that she was the head judge at this court centre. Happily I had done a few things against her before she became a judge, so I was hoping for a bit of slack. That said, I did not know, and did not want to predict the reaction to Her Honour being called "dear" in court, which I now viewed as inevitable. What was also nailed on, was a custodial sentence if she was convicted by the jury. Dunkirk Spirit and all that…

I went to get changed into my court robes and saw from the computer onto which all counsel have to log, that my opposite number was Daphne Edwards. Dapher's was a good mate, the daughter of a previous Commissioner of the Metropolitan Police, and possessor of a mind like a steel trap. Watching her being called "dear" was going to be good value too. I knocked on the ladies' robing room door and found Daphne in there alone. She waved me in. I explained that in essence her case was agreed, that I had a few questions for the OIC and that we should get it done, with a following wind, by tomorrow. The Judge had the usual two or three other matters, but if we got on promptly, we would be onto Mrs Tomlinson's evidence by late morning.

So, it proved. We started just before 11am, we raced through the schedules showing the regular inflow of money from the DWP and heard my learned friend and the OIC read out Gladys' interview between them. That at least was without elephant traps: she had kept it short and set out our defence clearly – that this was no more than human error. Amazingly she had not been asked what she spent the money on, so the fact that she was Cunard's most ardent supporter was not, yet, in the public domain.

At 12.30pm I called her to the witness box. Still armed with both hat and handbag she carefully walked down the steep steps from the dock, across the well of the court and up into the witness box. Before she took the oath HHJ Kaur said to her, "Please feel free to sit down, Mrs Tomlinson, just keep your voice up."

"Thank you, dear," she beamed. I couldn't resist looking at Her Honour, who was doing her best to suppress a smile as she glanced back at me.

I took her through her life story, happily married for 45 years, Reg's final illness and sad demise. Credit to Mrs T, she even managed a small weep at this point. She told us that she did not know how the pension system worked, that Reg had handled the finances and had given her an allowance to sort out the groceries for the two of them. She was doing well, although she did not let me down, managing to insert the word "dear" into every answer.

Then it was Daphne's turn. I sat wearing my "nothing to see here" innocent look which was designed not to alter even when the other side scored a direct and case-altering hit. Gladys was pressed on whether she really imagined that there would be no alteration to her finances when her husband died.

"No dear."

"What did you spend the money on?" she was asked.

Here we go.

"Well, I had always wanted to go on a cruise. So, I went on the QE2. I liked it so much, dear, that they started giving me Frequent Sailor Points." She was interrupted by the entire jury bursting out laughing. At her or with her? I wasn't sure. It was downhill from there. Daphne, unable to believe her luck, spent the remaining time until we broke off for lunch and a substantial percentage of the hour afterwards on the ins and outs of going cruising when you are in your early seventies, what was included in the price and what was extra.

"How did you afford it?" she was asked.

Not spotting the peril before her, Gladys replied, "Reg wasn't around anymore and I seemed to have more money, dear."

On it went, with my efforts to look vaguely bored by the proceedings, being sorely tested. Eventually the ordeal ended, and when I stood up and told Her Honour that I had no re-examination, Gladys actually looked disappointed. As Her Honour had no questions, she told her to resume her seat, and please take care with the steps ("Thank you, dear"). She made her way slowly back to the dock. At that point, Her Honour told us all that she had a sentence that she had to deal with at 3pm, we would discuss the law in the jury's absence and carry on in the morning. The legal discussion took seconds: the issue was dishonesty/did she know what the rules were, that she was entitled to a good character direction and the usual stuff. With that we rose.

I commandeered our room again and propelled Gladys into it. "How did I do?" she asked. I told her that she had not dropped the ball, that it was to be hoped that the jury liked her, and that I would deal with the ticklish issue of what the money was spent on in my final speech. As we were due to resume proceedings at 10am tomorrow I asked her to be at court no later than 9.30am. With a cheery "Thank you, dear" she went home.

We started bang on time for once. Despite what TV dramatists repeatedly suggest in the interests of I have no idea what, the order of events from here was set centuries ago and never altered. First the Prosecution final speech. Then the Defence, and then the summing up. In recent years, depending on the type of case and the judge, sometimes the summing up was split so the jury heard the law from the judge first, and then counsels' speeches, then the judge's summary of the evidence. What had not changed, and nor was it going to, was that the Defence always got the last word. In a case this straightforward, there was no need to split the summing up, so Daphne was up to the plate first. I was expecting a measured, even kind, more-in-sorrow-than-in-anger speech to the effect that while Mrs Tomlinson could, indeed should, attract every sympathy, the sad truth was that she had knowingly defrauded the State, and that explanation was the only proper interpretation of the evidence. Which is precisely what we got, all the more deadly because it was delivered with charm and a smile.

I sat there for twenty-five minutes willing her to shut up and sit down, marvelling at how utterly lethal she was. Her usual fare, prosecuting London's armed robbers for the Flying Squad, had had the effect of sharpening her game.

Finally, it was my turn. I did not make a habit of praising my client to the skies, on the basis that a jury would be expecting that, and my usual tactic of fighting the case on enemy territory by pointing out all the flaws in the Prosecution evidence was rendered redundant by our accepting that she had received the money. So, taking for granted my hope that the jury already liked her and were sympathetic to her was accurate, I decided to deal head-on with the issue of where the money had gone. I pointed out that if she had simply banked it, we would still be here, although that might have speeded up repayment. That she had spent it all, and spent it on having a good time was actually irrelevant to the issue in the case: had she known what her obligations were, and was this no more than an unfortunate mistake? If so, end of case. You can divine this, members of the jury, from her very appearance: coming to court in her smartest clothes, being one of that generation of ladies who never went out without a hat. While it was not a blanket rule, it was by no means unheard of for tasks to be divided up in a marriage, so when she says that Reg dealt with the money and gave her enough to sort out the domestic finances, it was hardly obvious nonsense. They all looked interested, a few nodded and about half made sporadic notes. The Prosecution would have to prove to you that her case was total rubbish, and on the available evidence they could not. Thus, there was a reasonable doubt. Proper verdict: not guilty.

The summing up was a model of brevity and fairness. The law you take from me, treat her good character very much in her favour, the Prosecution say this, the Defence say that, this is a classic jury case for you to decide whether this lady has deliberately embarked on fraud. They were in retirement by 11.30am.

The conference room was busy so I walked Gladys down to a quiet corner of the building. She asked me, not unreasonably, the one question I could not answer, which was how long would the jury be? She looked as chipper as at any time since I first met her. My insides, by contrast, were churning. A bit like a doctor, it helped to be dispassionate, so when things went wrong it did not get to you. Otherwise one would go nuts. Some clients though, you could not help but like, and Gladys was one of them. Had I done enough? What had I missed? Yes, and nothing were the answers to those questions. It did not help. Nor did the fact that Her Honour Judge Kaur was nothing if not a professional, and it was wise to assume that sentiment would play no part in any sentencing exercise. Going down to the cells to see your client after you have lost was part of the job. Going down to the cells to see your seventy-nine-year-old client who had never been in trouble before, was not the ambition of the week. So, we waited.

At 3.35pm the tannoy announced that all parties in the case of Tomlinson should go to Court 1. Sitting outside court, as she had been all day, was Gladys, quite serene, but also alone. There had been no children and she told me that she did not wish to burden the wider family with this little local difficulty. Worse, she had announced in our first conference that she had every faith in my ability, so would not be bringing a bag of toiletries and personal effects to court, because she was not going to prison. She was working completely without a net. In we went and there followed the usual delay as everyone was assembled. HHJ Kaur told her that she did not have to stand to receive the verdict. I hoped that I was doing a better job than it felt, of disguising my nerves.

"Members of the jury, do you find Gladys Iris Tomlinson guilty or not guilty of fraud?"

"Not guilty."

I could hold my pen but there was little point as I was shaking so much. I stood and asked Her Honour that she be discharged from the dock and that a Defendant's Costs Order be made in a sum my solicitors would supply. "Yes" to both requests, and the Judge went on to thank the jury for their time, pointing out again that this was just the sort of case that juries should have to decide. While she did not know what the future held for them, they went with her thanks and would they please go with the usher. With that she rose from the Bench.

Outside court Gladys looked much the same as she had throughout. While her liberty was no longer under threat, the ticklish business of owing a large sum to the DWP would not be going away. She brushed that aside, thanked me profusely, left me with a smacker on my right cheek and walked back into her life. I went for a much-needed pint in the pub across the road, joined by Daphne a few minutes later, who congratulated me on the win. And slowly my blood pressure returned to normal. Phew!

8

Saturday morning was another fine, warm day and I had a good quick run to Norfolk. As I pulled into the drive, the reception committee of dogs greeted me, followed shortly afterwards by the children and then the lady of the house. I lugged the large shopping bag containing Akely Motorsport accounts out of the passenger seat and handed it over. She looked a little better. She was still very pale, but I was beginning to realise that was at least somewhat natural – she had white-blonde hair, and eyes such a pale grey they seemed almost translucent. But she did at least look like she might have slept at some point.

We headed into the kitchen as the children ran about chasing the dogs, giggling. I said how pleased I was that she was at least managing.

"I'm coping," she said. "Most of the time. It's pretty bleak at night, and I don't sleep much. The children are helping – they need me to keep it together, so I do."

"I can see that," I said. "Has there been any word from the coroner?"

"The cause of death has been given as blunt trauma to the head. They haven't released the body yet. I want to have the funeral. Bill's parents are at their wits' end. I don't know how to speed things up."

"I can ask the coroner's officer on your behalf, if you want."

She closed her eyes for a second, and then smiled. "Thank you, James. How will I ever repay you?"

"Completely unnecessary," I said. "It's the least I can do. Now, changing the subject a bit – do you want me to show you those payments from Cayman?"

"Good idea." She retrieved the bank statement folders and I pointed out the incoming money.

"Do you have any customers who bank in Cayman?" I asked.

"No," she replied. "I've wracked my brains, and I can't think of anyone."

"And I suspect that the main attraction of that account is how untraceable it is. You could try emailing the bank, but I'd bet my house that they'll tell you to shove it."

"I'd say the same if I thought I'd have a house to bet in six months' time," said Claire.

"Nonsense," I said. "You're going to be absolutely fine. Come on, let's see what you're working with."

We headed outside. One of the fancy trucks was at Oulton Park, but its mate was gleaming in the yard. Claire showed me round the cab, and then the various sections of the trailer. Everything was immaculate, including the tools in the tool racks; no oil or grease anywhere. Bill, it seemed, liked cleanliness. It was all hugely impressive.

From there we went into the barn, which was used as a large four-bay workshop. Again, everything was immaculate. Work in progress included a Ford Falcon, a Mustang, a race MGB and, to my surprise, a race prepared Austin A35. "Whose is that?" I asked.

"Ah, that belongs to the grandson of a friend of Tolly's. He's mad keen on historic racing and has entered the A35 Academy series."

I knew of it: as an inexpensive way of going racing for novices it had few equals, and was very popular. Very much a people's car of the 1950s, the few rusty survivors had been mouldering away in sheds, garages and barns for decades. Now all of a sudden, they were being hauled out, repaired, lowered and stuffed full of go-faster bits, ready for a glorious second coming. Everybody cheered the entertaining, if not exactly period-correct, sight at the Goodwood Revival of A35s chasing and beating Jaguars.

I went over and had a look at it. It was mint, with not a scratch or scuff on it. Typical Akely Motorsport preparation then.

"Has it won anything?" I asked.

"Well, Freddie only started racing this season, so he took it gently to start with. I gather he won at Brands Hatch a few weeks ago."

We pottered about the barn. In one corner was an almost exact replica of Terry's office, with room for desk, telephone and four chairs against the wall. The difference was that it was as tidy as everything else. Instead of a mountain of paper, the desk had a blotter and two trays, one for "in" and one for "out". Above the desk were rows of lever-arch files. I took one down and leafed through it; it was a daily record of work done, with suppliers' bills and carbon copies of the invoices sent out by Claire.

"Was he always so hot on tidiness?" I asked.

"He said that it made things easier," she replied. "He wouldn't be wasting time trying to find a spanner or the relevant paperwork or whatever. It would just be there. We all just fell into line. The young mechanics when they started here would leave tools lying on the top of the benches. Bill never said anything, just picked them up and put them away at the end of each day. They got the message soon enough."

Claire had sunk down onto a bench as she'd been talking, and so I sat down next to her.

"Have you given any thought to what you'll do in the medium term?" I asked.

She nodded. "I'd like to keep it going. If we don't I'll have to sell up and move – I can't afford to live here without an income. The problem is, the business was about Bill. It was *his* driving that made the cars seem quick, *his* ambition that got us into Europe, *his* skill with all the preparation that gave us our reputation. The boys are good, and Tolly is excellent, but neither he nor I have the skills to make this work in the long term."

"I'm sorry," I said. "Let's talk about something else. Who's at Oulton Park?"

"Tolly, Ted and Michael," she replied. "They're running Max De Vries's Alfa in a one-hour race, and a Mustang for a new Italian client in the same event."

"Time Max and I had a chat, I think," I said. "I'll go up to Oulton Park tomorrow. By the way – do you know where Max stays when he's in the UK?"

"He has a flat in London somewhere," she replied. "I can get the address for you."

We walked back to the house. Claire insisted on offering me dinner, which we ate with the children in the kitchen. The children still seemed subdued, but when asked questions about their schoolwork and friends opened up a little. After dinner Claire took me on a short tour of the garden, and the children played with a set of skittles. It was such a peaceful evening; they were such nice people. The crashing unfairness of the whole thing haunted me all the way back to London.

-

Although I wished the circumstances were better, I wasn't unhappy about heading up to Oulton Park; racing or watching, it was my favourite circuit. As the weather forecast for the next five days was unseasonably fine, I elected to drive up there in the TR, partly to enjoy the racing, but mainly to speak to Max. I now had his address in London, but this was going to be a strange conversation at best, and I'd rather have it with plenty of other people around.

As I rumbled over the bridge to the car park at Oulton, I could hear cars whistling past underneath. It had the same effect on me now that it had had when I started watching racing as a teenager: I was obviously missing the best stuff.

I headed for the paddock and the Akely Motor Sport transporter in the hope of catching a word with Tolly. When I got there it was deserted, and the reason was immediately clear: the Mustang and the Alfa were out practising, and Tolly was in the pits. Although I didn't have the right passes, if you looked like you belonged there you could usually get to the pit wall – security at club meetings was nothing like that at Goodwood.

Tolly was easy to spot: no one else had dressed as if for a regimental dinner. He smiled as I joined him, although since he was busy with the stopwatches I did not interrupt. I glanced at his time sheet. Santo Monteriggione appeared to be in first, and a commendable half a second a lap behind him was Max. Good driving, given the large power disadvantage, but Oulton had always been a drivers' track. I watched the cars howl past, feeling envious. When the session ended I asked Tolly if I could speak to Max in the truck.

I got back to the truck just as the drivers were getting out of their cars. Both were wreathed in sweat as they pulled off gloves, helmets and balaclavas and unzipped their race suits. We all drifted into the hospitality area.

I didn't know Max that well and had last spoken to him on the start line at Goodwood just after Bill's accident, but when I carefully drifted his way he smiled and waved me over.

"Why aren't you out today, James?" he said, taking a sip of water.

"Oh, the car hasn't been touched since the Six Hours – it needs brakes, tyres and an oil change, at least. At this rate I *might* get out for the October meeting at Castle Combe."

Max laughed. "Hard luck," he said. "Well, I hope you make it – Castle Combe should be fun."

I looked around us. No-one else was nearby – Santo and the boys had gone to look at something under the Alfa's bonnet.

"Look, Max, can I ask you a favour?"

Max smiled. "Of course," he said. "What can I do for you?"

"Well – look, after Bill's death, Claire Akely called me, wanting to talk it through. She's in a bad way, as you'd imagine, and – well, she says you had a big argument with Bill in the summer, and she can't work out what happened. D'you mind telling me what it was about?"

Max's smiled faltered a little, but didn't entirely disappear. "I do mind a bit, old chap – it's private."

"I know, but – "

"Trust me," Max said. "It was just a stupid argument." His expression softened a little. "I know Claire must be obsessing over detail, but this one isn't important. Promise." He downed the rest of his water. "Got to run. See you about."

He turned on his heel and left. I followed him, more slowly, and watched him enter the circuit cafe.

Tolly came over, and I explained what had happened.

"Can you throw any more light on it?" I asked.

"I promise you, I've been thinking about it a lot. The only thing I can think of is that Ted was standing nearer to them – he might have heard part of the row. Why don't you speak to him?"

I nodded, and Tolly beckoned Ted over. "Ted, James here wants to know about what you heard when Bill and Max De Vries had that row. James is a lawyer, and he's giving Claire a hand with things, since he understands cars as well. We're just trying to figure things out."

"How much of the argument did you hear?" I asked.

"We'd just come back from a meeting," Ted said. "I forget which one, but we'd all been together in the cab. I was unloading the cars and tools, so was in and out of the truck and the barn. I didn't pay attention to it to start with. It wasn't like Bill to argue with anyone, so it wasn't until they started shouting I realised it was a fight."

"Do you remember anything of what either of them said?" I asked.

"No, not really," he replied. "Well…thinking about it, I reckon I heard Bill say 'that was the last time', and it seemed to make Mr De Vries even angrier. Actually, that was the moment he stormed off."

"Do you have any idea what they meant?" I asked.

"No. The trouble is, because I was going in and out, and because I didn't want them thinking I was eavesdropping, I was actively trying *not* to listen. And I didn't think it my place to ask Bill what it was about afterwards, what with me being the most junior member of staff." He looked unhappy. "I'm sorry."

"Don't be," I said. "You've been very helpful. I appreciate it." He shrugged and went back to what he had been doing.

Tolly and I looked at each other, both baffled. What had Bill been up to that he was not prepared to do again? Did this have anything to do with the rogue payments? What about the search by customs? What on earth was going on here?

-

This was a forty-five-minute race with, in theory, a driver change. If you were driving alone, which was permitted, you had to get out and run round the car before getting back in and resume racing. I joined Tolly on the pit wall once again, and watched the race unfold from there.

Santo blasted into the lead and was a length up as the field poured into Old Hall, the first right hander. Max, having started sixth, was down to tenth as he passed us, and entered Old Hall on the grass. As they came round for a second time, Santo was still in the lead, but Max was well down the field and had a large dent in the driver's door to boot. As it settled down he started to make progress, but either his touch seemed to have deserted him or he was on particularly muscular form, because ten laps in he came past us with a crunched nearside front corner, and a few laps later the car was covered in mud. As the race neared its end it occurred to me that it would probably not be helpful for me or the Akely's if Max found me still about on his return. I found the Triumph and made a tactical withdrawal.

9

The business of the week was in Lincoln, representing a Northern Irishman who had lost it in a bar and more or less demolished the place. Evidently the scene at the time was like a Randolph Scott movie, including people jumping out of a first-floor window in their eagerness to escape my client; he was charged with inflicting grievous bodily harm, affray and criminal damage. The defence to this allegation was "they fucking deserved it", with a light veneer of self-defence. On the face of it, he was toast. However, his drinking buddy and co-defendant had been given such a pasting that he had suffered brain damage, and between that and the generally crap quality of evidence given by drunk people, I had just about enough to work with. By the end of the week, I'd managed to wangle a "not guilty".

Another victory for justice.

The relatively routine nature of the week's work gave me plenty of time to think about the whole Akely problem. By Friday afternoon, I'd decided to at least try and tackle it from the other end. My great friend Tony Allbright, sometime university flat mate and de facto brother, was a senior prosecutor for HM Customs. I called him and after we had chatted about our families, I asked him if he could tee up a drink with one of his investigators.

"Yes, but you're buying the first two rounds, James," Tony said. "I don't know what you're up to, but it smells like trouble."

Tony played a blinder; through the magic of the phrase "free pints", he managed to collect up a senior customs officer named Clive and a couple of in-house prosecution solicitors and drag them to the pub. I bided my time until the others were nattering about family and holidays, and got Clive's attention.

"Can I pick your brains about something?" I asked.

Clive grinned. "Tony mentioned you might do this," he said. "Go on, fire away."

Over the next pint, I outlined the whole story, focusing on the strange business with customs. He looked interested, and asked sensible questions. When I'd finished, he nodded.

"Well, I can't give you operational information," he said. "I can't give you classified information. In theory I can't help at all. But…"

"But?"

"But my brother is a senior investigator at Dover. I can ask him to divulge what *is* disclosable. Or, rather, what he's prepared to tell me."

"Can you tell me whether there was a tip-off about the transporter?" I asked.

"In theory, no," Clive said. "In practice, I'll tell you as much as I can."

"You're a gentleman and a scholar," I said. "My round, I think."

I left them still putting the world to rights, wandered down to Temple tube station and caught the District Line to Hammersmith. Half asleep and more than a few drinks down, I walked against the traffic down Beedon Road, part of the one-way system that feeds eastbound traffic into the

Hammersmith Broadway roundabout. At that time the road was quiet. Coming towards me was a black cab and a dark coloured car which I noticed absently didn't have any lights on. The taxi passed by, but all at once the car revved its engine, mounted the pavement, and drove at speed straight at me. I twisted to my left and pressed myself into a shop doorway; the front wing bashed my right leg and bundled me backwards down the pavement.

The car, engine still racing, carried on down the pavement for a few yards, dropped back onto the road, went through a red light onto the Broadway and disappeared.

I was winded and in increasing pain from my right thigh. I lay there for a bit, trying to work out what worked and what didn't. I started to sit up and found myself looking at the taxi driver, identifiable by the badge on a halter round his neck.

"Farkin' 'ell mate," he said. "That was fackin' deliberate. I saw it in my mirror. He was going for you. Who've you upset?"

"No idea," I mumbled, weakly. "My leg hurts."

"Not fackin' surprised, mate," he said. "Let me help you up." He put his hands under my armpits and hauled me to my feet. "Where'd you live?"

"Just around the corner. Tabor Road." I tried to put weight on my right leg, but it gave way immediately.

"You should get that checked out at the hospital. I'll run you down there."

He carried me to his cab, which he'd left with the engine running and the driver's door open, and drove me to the A and E department of the Charing Cross Hospital. He flagged down the first policeman he saw (which didn't take long in an A and E), told him firmly what he had seen, and flatly refused to take any money for the fare.

"Put twenty quid into Help for Heroes," he said. With a wave and an expression that said he'd finally seen everything, he went off into the night. I never even got his name.

The next few hours were a blur of nurses, doctors, radiographers and police officers. It was two o'clock the following morning before I was discharged from hospital, having been told that I had a badly bruised leg, one broken rib, some cuts to my hands and abrasions to my right torso. I would also be needing a new suit. The police were kind, if business-like, and we agreed that they would call round later that morning for me to make a formal statement.

I took another cab home, and was helped inside by the driver. I went upstairs on my bottom, one step at a time, ran a hot bath and took stock of the damage. For jockeys and rugby players, this was a normal part of life. For a soft southerner who had somehow never broken a bone in his body, it was bloody unpleasant. I lay in the bath until it was nearly cold, dried myself lying on the bathroom floor and crawled up the final few stairs into bed, having swallowed as many painkillers as I thought I could get away with. Sleep proved elusive.

When I decided at about eight o'clock that lying about in bed would achieve nothing, I made the return journey to the bath and had another good soaking. This time it appeared to help, and by mid-morning I was hobbling about, leg throbbing. My plan had been to drive up to my parents and do something about the brakes on the Cortina in preparation for the upcoming meeting at Castle Combe. That would have to wait, but a bit of maternal TLC wouldn't go amiss.

The police arrived at eleven o'clock, and making my statement took about forty-five minutes. I didn't feel it necessary to mention who I had been with earlier in the evening, and I wasn't at all sure that what had happened was connected to the whole Akely situation. If it was a planned attempt to kill me or shut me up, how can they possibly have known that I would be walking down that road at that exact moment? Had the car been lying in wait? I had only seen it when it was on the move driving behind my Good Samaritan's taxi. Even worse, as the adult version of the proud child who had known the make and model of every car on the British roads from the age of four, I wasn't even sure what make of car it was. Useless. My younger self would have been appalled. While I wasn't sure that Beedon Road was covered by CCTV, Hammersmith Broadway definitely was, so at least there was some hope we might be able to find out.

I drove gingerly to Essex, arriving in time for a late lunch. My mother, not normally known for unnecessary sympathy, nevertheless sprinted out of the back door of the house, having seen from the kitchen window my efforts to get out of the car and walk into the house.

"What have you done, darling?"

"Inside," I said through gritted teeth, and thrust my overnight bag at her.

Once installed on the sofa in front of the fire, with a glass of Rioja in hand and fending off the benign attention of the dog, I explained what had happened the night before.

"Have you told the police?"

"Yes," I replied.

"Do you think it's something to do with one of your cases?" she asked.

I explained that the incidents of unhappy punters attacking either counsel or judges were vanishingly few in number. The only one I could recall was the prosecution counsel being hit on the back of the head with a brick while walking between Wood Green Crown Court and the Tube, and that hadn't been serious. Even the IRA had never attacked a judge, although I knew that plenty had had Special Branch protection for a while. Punters in England were savvy enough to realise that attacking your own barrister was idiotic, and attacking the prosecution barrister, though no doubt a satisfying daydream, wasn't worth the hassle.

"It could have been an accident, or a drunk driver," I said. "Don't worry about it, Mum."

Lunch was brought to the sofa, and afterwards I managed a snooze in front of the fire, periodically interrupted by the dog nudging her nose under my left elbow. As the afternoon drifted into the evening I had another hot bath, which had the effect of lessening the pain but increasing the depth of the reds, blues and yellows on my right side. I looked like a Turner painting. Whisky, I discovered, was an effective anaesthetic, and suddenly I was a teenager again, with my mother producing huge quantities of food and my father being, by turns, slightly acerbic and very funny. I went to bed early, no longer needing to take the stairs one at a time on my bottom. Progress.

When I came downstairs the following morning, I found that my phone was teeming with message alerts. The first was from DC Perkins of Hammersmith Police, who wanted me to call back as a matter of urgency. Next was my neighbour Chris, who said that he had been up early to walk the dog and had therefore seen that every front window of my place had been smashed. There were two more similar messages from people I knew less well.

I called DC Perkins, and he told me much the same thing as Chris.

"One bit of good news, though," he said. "We've got that footage from the Broadway. The car that hit you was a black or dark blue Ford Focus."

"Well that's something," I said. I could hear the weariness in my own voice.

"Are you sure that there is something that you are not telling me?" he asked. "Friday night could just about be a drunken accident. This definitely is you being targeted."

I explained how infrequently criminals came after barristers, and didn't mention the whole Akely situation. Hell, I wasn't even sure it *was* a situation. I knew that on my street there was no CCTV, so whoever had done this was not going to be apprehended that way, but I was reassured that the police were doing house-to-house calls.

After hanging up, I called Chris. Having lived in W6 for decades he knew everyone and everything; he put me on to an emergency glazier, who agreed, for a stellar fee, to abandon his plans for Sunday lunch with his family and come out and do something about filling in the holes.

My parents, who were listening to my end of these conversations while appearing to be studying sections of the *Sunday Times*, made it clear that they were now properly worried about my safety. Not having ever been in this position before, I was inclined to agree with them, but I didn't think that sharing that view with two people in their early seventies was a great idea. They agreed that hiding achieved nothing, so helped me back to the car, and I headed home.

When I got back the glazier was hard at it, so I let him in and left him to get on with it. There wasn't much in the fridge, so lunch was a cheese sandwich and a medicinal glass of wine while I pondered my next move. As I was on light duties the following day, I decided to make good on my promise to bother the coroner's officer about getting Bill's body released to the family. Thinking of it made me think of Claire. Before I entirely realised what I was doing, I had dialled her number.

"James," she said. "It's nice to hear from you. How are you doing?"

We chatted lightly for a little bit. Claire was easy to talk to; she laughed at my descriptions of my clients, and asked interesting questions about the cases.

"It's the clothes that always got me," she said. "I know it's all very serious, but I can't see how anyone can talk about life and death with a wig on."

I laughed. "Well, it's not like drivers look much better," I said. "We're all wearing so much flame proof fabric we look like the Michelin man."

Claire laughed too. "You're not wrong," she said. "I used to tell Bill that he…" Her voice trailed off. "Strange to think he died in it. I wish he'd at least been able to put his clothes back on, you know? He had this lucky tie he wore on race days…I suppose Goodwood still have it, with the rest of his things. Or the police, maybe."

The tone of her voice was unbearably sad. "How are you holding up?" I asked.

"Oh, OK I suppose," she said. "I have nights where I don't sleep. The worst thing is that everything is on hold. We need closure. Bill's parents are going downhill rapidly. Mine are in a state of constant upset. The children keep asking when they can say goodbye to their daddy, and I can't tell them anything. It's horrible."

"I'm so sorry, Claire," I said. "I'll chase it tomorrow. How are things going with the business?"

"Michael has handed in his notice. Well, I say that – he walked up to the back door on Friday, said he was leaving, and could I pay him what we owe him? I said that he needed to give notice, to which he replied that this was it. I was furious. He can be paid at the end of his notice period, in three months' time."

"What about the clients? Are they still on board?"

"Max De Vries had a shocker at Oulton Park, as I think you know. What on earth did you say to him?"

"I just asked him about the row between him and Bill."

"Tolly said that he came into the paddock, flung off the belts, found his kit bag and got into his road car, all without saying a word," she said. "He left no instructions about what we're supposed to do with the damage to the car, and I've been unable to get hold of him this week. It's just sitting here in a shed round the back, covered in mud, looking rather sorry for itself. As for the others – Santo and Timo – I haven't heard from them. We have two more meetings, Castle Combe and Estoril in Portugal, and then it's winter. It should be a quiet period, but during the last two we were frantically rebuilding cars. It was all going so well. I just don't know what to do for the best in the long term."

"What about a manager?" I asked.

"That is what Tolly is now," she said. "He looks and acts years younger than his actual age, so could keep going for the next two or three years. The real issue is that if you cut the head off anything, eventually it will die. I'm not about to take up motor racing or automotive engineering. I suppose the best course will be to wind it up amicably while there's still a customer base and goodwill, and move to somewhere smaller. I like it here, though. I suppose we won't have to move far."

"Not something you need to decide today, though?"

"No," she replied. "But soon. Soon."

-

I switched on my computer and found, hiding in the spam box, an email from Guy De Bruyen, the clerk of the course at Spa. Would I mind calling him? With the glazier still doing his thing, now would be as good a time as any.

"Monsieur," I said. "It's James Westerfeld. You asked me to call you? I apologise for the delay, but your email went into my junk box."

He laughed. "It is not a problem. I'm very glad for you to ring me. We have an enquiry coming up in a few days, and I would like you to be a witness for the circuit."

"When's the hearing?" I asked.

"Is on Friday of this coming week. Do you have Skype? We would be very happy for you to be on your computer, rather than travel all the way to Verviers," he said.

"I'll be delighted to help, if I can. But you should know that although I was the first car to arrive, I didn't see what caused it."

"I realise this," he said. "We have good CCTV at Spa, and we can see where you were when it started. This is a state inquest, not a Belgian FIA enquiry. I have been told that the judge may have some questions for you."

"Then I'll be there," I said. "What time and on which day is the hearing?" The rest of the conversation was taken up by the logistics of checking mobile numbers, email addresses and Skype addresses.

Having put the phone down to him, the glazier started making I'll-be-off-now noises. He handed me a hand-written invoice, and having survived my minor heart attack at the price, I paid him. I had never been more glad to sink onto my sofa with a whisky.

10

On Monday I was out of court because on Tuesday we had the preliminary hearing in the upcoming murder. While most of the morning was taken up with preparation for that, I spent a good hour and a half on the telephone attempting to contact both Goodwood circuit and the Coroner's Officer. Both seem to speak fluent bureaucrat.

As I was dealing with a serving police officer at the Coroner's Office, and as I was representing the family as their lawyer, they could (eventually) see the basis for my call. It took longer than it should have done, but when he opened up, I was told that the cause of death had been established: blunt trauma to the head due to the seatbelt mounting snapping during the collision with the barriers. They had run the usual toxicology tests and nothing untoward was found.

I pointed out that the family were anxious for closure and wanted Bill's body returned to them as soon as possible, but, I imagined out loud, they had, *of course* taken tissue samples should other lines of enquiry become relevant? Answer: of course. Heart, cornea, liver, kidney and spleen.

That settled, I organised a private ambulance to take Bill's body back to Norfolk the day after tomorrow, and then called Claire and helped her organise an undertaker.

Having got as far as I was going to with that, I turned my attention to Goodwood itself. They proved a tougher nut to crack; mainly, I thought, because while police officers dealt with either prosecution or defence lawyers all the time, the powers that be at the circuit did not. It took longer than it should have done merely to persuade them that I *was* acting on behalf of the Akely family. It didn't help that my real contact there was John Russell, who wasn't a Goodwood employee. The Revival Meeting was put on by Goodwood, and the boss was His Grace the Duke, but the *organisation* of the actual races was done by the British Automobile Racing Club, the senior figures of which were volunteers and not part of the permanent Goodwood set-up, and on, and on, and on.

After an interminable amount of this, I gave up, telephoned Goodwood House, and asked to speak to The Duke's personal assistant. The very business-like Torquil Evans-Jones asked how he could help.

"Mrs Akely was wondering where Bill's holdall had got to. Originally it would have contained helmet, overalls and boots, but as he was wearing all that when he was taken to hospital, it would have had his street clothes in."

"Have the family not had it back?"

"They've not. And since it contained some personal items…"

"No, of course." Torquil paused. "Let me look into it. It'll either be here or with the police, I suspect."

"Thank you," I said. "I appreciate this a lot."

"Not at all," Torquil said. "We've agonised over this for the last few weeks. Incidentally, please let us know when the funeral will be – His Grace would wish to attend."

I didn't bother Claire with that detail quite yet. The last thing she needed was a Duke to worry about.

The plan for tomorrow was to spend the morning at Lincoln Crown Court speaking to the client about his situation and then have the actual hearing at 2 o'clock. Mr Andreas Bularenko was one of the sizeable eastern European community which had grown up in the last ten years in and around Boston. Like many of his compadrés Mr Bularenko worked on the land for one of the gangmasters who had a lock on agricultural work in the area. Without this labour force, few of the brussell sprouts, cauliflowers, daffodils or similar crops would ever get pulled out of the ground. The work was seasonal, back breaking and poorly paid. The money, such as it was, was stretched thinner by the industrial levels of alcohol consumption that they all seemed to indulge in. Like many, Mr Bularenko had moved his wife and children here, but that did not seem to put a brake on the booze bill. She, as far as I could tell, matched him glass for glass. It did not pay to enquire too closely as to the arrangements for child care of an evening, chez Bularenko. Six weeks before it had been Mr Bularenko's birthday, seen as an excuse to give his elbow a proper workout. The party started as a kids' barbecue at around noon, and was well behaved enough. At around 7pm the children were being ushered indoors and other people started to arrive at his garden. By 9pm there was a full-on party taking place, and of the thirty or so guests present, he knew fewer than half of them. At about 11pm an argument broke out between three of the men present. All were hammered. Two of their wives got involved and the women, also in tatters, started fighting. Within seconds there was an ongoing brawl which spilled into the street. Mr Bularenko, anxious not to upset his neighbours had gone out onto the street to try and referee the situation. He was promptly attacked by one of the men, one Aleksy Kowalski, who took exception to him being there. Andreas, now well down the third bottle of vodka, found that his mediation skills had deserted him and punched

Kowalski in the face. It was the Defence case that, at this stage, Mr Kowlski produced a knife. This part of the incident was caught on the council CCTV, and while one could see Mr Kowalski put his hand in his pocket, you could not see what, if anything, he pulled out. What you could see, all too clearly, was Mr Bularenko stepping back, taking a two-pace run-up and hitting Mr Kowalski full in the face. Hard. Unsurprisingly, and almost certainly already unconscious, Kowalski fell backwards like a caber. His head hit the concrete pavement and the impact caused a brain injury from which he died two days later.

The police and ambulance were on the scene quickly, and Mr Bularenko was arrested immediately. The scene was searched thoroughly. No knife was found. Some idea of how inebriated he had been can be derived from the fact that he could not be interviewed by the police for two days. He had answered their questions, said that he was attacked first, and that he had acted in reasonable self-defence throughout. The purpose of the hearing was to take his plea, set the trial date, deal with the case administration and, for my solicitor and I to meet the client properly, get used to him, get him used to us and both guide him through the whole process, as well as taking his detailed instructions as to what he said about all this.

We were with him most of the morning. At 2pm sharp the case was called into court. We were before HHJ Hines. He took the plea (not guilty), set the trial date, ordered the prosecution to serve the full papers in good time and generally cut through to what mattered. Better yet, he asked if I wanted a QC. Normally that application had to be done in writing, but he waved that requirement away and granted it on the spot.

Murders have a cachet at the criminal bar that dates back to the days of capital murder. As something of an amateur historian, I have read many accounts of the lengths defence counsels would go to on their client's behalf. One defence silk (QC) was up until 3 o'clock in the morning working out what he might say on his client's behalf, when the client had pleaded guilty to murder. In those days there was no discretion as to sentence. The judge had to pass the death sentence, once guilt had been established, either by a plea of guilty or a finding of guilt by a jury, all one could hope for was that the plea of guilty would later persuade the Home Secretary to commute the sentence. So, to an extent, it did not matter what one did or did not say on one's client's behalf, as it would not make the slightest difference to the outcome. But that did not prevent barristers agonising into the night about their clients. That sort of pressure was, happily, a thing of the past, but being instructed in a murder remained big news.

-

The next week was occupied by a case which really highlighted the glamour of a criminal barrister's life: a three-day stint on a shoplifting case at Croydon Crown Court. Shopliftings are buggers to contest. If you walk out of a shop without paying, there's a slim list of acceptable reasons as to how or why that might have happened. Added to that, my client was a middle-aged lady who I'd represented twice before, both times also for shoplifting. I did my best to wave the flag for her, but the position was pretty hopeless. After a summing up that left one in not too much doubt what the judge thought about her, the jury retired at 11.45am.

While I was having a coffee and praying somewhat listlessly that the jury might have been asleep through literally all of the evidence, my phone rang. It was Clive, the customs official.

"I spoke to my brother, as I said I would." He was clearly not messing around with pleasantries. "Before I say anything, though – you understand this conversation never happened."

I did.

"Alright, then. The reason the William Akely Motorsport transporter was searched *was* the result of a tip-off. They were expecting to find drugs in the lorry, although they didn't."

"That would explain the thoroughness of the search, then," I replied.

"Yes. I gather they were surprised not to find anything. Also, and this might interest you – the Bank of Cayman is very much on our radar. They're an elaborate front for American organised crime. Having a bank account with them more of less guarantees a criminal background. On a no-promises basis, if you give me the account numbers of the paying accounts of the two rogue payments, I might – *might* – be able to tell you who paid those sums of money."

"Clive, you're a star!" I gave him my email address and rang off, just in time for my client to be found guilty. So, it goes.

-

Friday brought an early start and a sheaf of cases at Portsmouth, but I was finished with the morning work by 12.50pm, so hid myself away in one of the conference rooms on the top floor and called Guy De Bruyen. At exactly 1pm my computer lit up and I was greeted with a scene familiar to all barristers: three avocats sitting in a row, and in the corner of the image the judge.

The judge introduced all three avocats and explained who they were representing, and there was some procedural faff about Belgian law which I tried relatively hard to follow. Eventually, we got down to it.

I explained that I had just started my stint, that I was trying to catch an Alfa Romeo, that as I passed the old pits, going down the hill towards Eau Rouge I had been passed by two Lotus Elans and an AC Cobra. The Cobra had overtaken the two Lotuses going up the hill to Les Combes. I was in the process of overtaking the Alfa as I approached Pouhon Corner, and at that point the three quicker cars were out of sight. As I rounded the first part of the corner, I saw a scene of devastation, with the AC upside down and on fire, one Lotus missing its nose in the wall, and the Lotus of Jeremy Smith bouncing upside down along the debris fence on the outside of the circuit shedding bits of bodywork as it went.

"Could you guess how this might have happened, M. Westerfeld?"

I nodded. "If two cars are running very close together it's possible for the tyres to rub together. Sometimes that's all they do. But sometimes they interlock. The forces involved are enough to lift a car off its wheels, and it has been known for a car to be turned upside down in these circumstances. In the year 2000 at the Goodwood Revival, a start line accident in similar circumstances had caused a front engined Ferrari to barrel roll and throw the driver clean out of the car. He, fortunately, landed on a tyre wall which had saved his life. So, if, here, one of the Lotuses attempted to pass the Cobra on the way in to Pouhon Corner, and the second Lotus was *right* behind the other two cars, he too may have been caught up in the accident. I have heard that the corner was covered by CCTV, so that would help the court."

"Monsieur Westerfeld," said the judge, "Have you seen the CCTV?"

"Your Honour, no I have not."

"If we can show it to you over the link we are on, the court would be grateful if you could watch it. We can see what it shows us. But you are a racing driver. You may see something that is important to you, but not obvious to us lawyers."

The court turned the camera that had been pointing at the judge to a large wall mounted screen. The first shot was looking back up the hill with the entry to Pouhon in the bottom right-hand corner of the screen. It showed the three cars running in line, in the order AC, Lotus, Lotus. As they entered the braking zone, *both* Lotuses moved up the inside of the Cobra with a view to passing it. The AC is a bigger, heavier car than the Lotus, so it would have to brake earlier. The move was completely fair enough for the first Lotus, but more ambitious for the second. Jeremy Smith was driving the first Lotus. Everything still looked OK when the three cars went out of view. Coming down the hill towards the camera were the Alfa and me. The next shot was again looking back towards where the cars were coming from, with the camera positioned about half way through the corner. As the three cars come into view the AC was just ahead. It turned in against both of the Lotuses, apparently unaware that they were there, attempting a pass. As the nearside of the Cobra hit the offside of the Smith Lotus, the AC reared up onto the two offside wheels. Part of the AC caught something low down on the Smith Lotus and flicked the whole car up into the air. It then somersaulted and barrel rolled into, onto and along the top of the barrier until it was out of view. Meanwhile the Cobra and the second Lotus effectively fell over each other. The Lotus heading straight for the wall, impacting hard enough to have its nose knocked off. The Cobra continued its slow-motion roll, landing upside down. There was a brief pause before a puff of white smoke in the area of the fuel filler turned orange as the car caught fire. Both drivers were out of their cars in short order, although if their tottering walks were any guide, both were a bit dazed.

The last scene was the next camera along, again with the cars coming towards it. This was less clear, except that it showed the Smith Elan coming to rest, me stopping my car, getting out and running towards him. The shot was then partially obscured by the figures of the three marshals racing back up the track away from the camera to deal with it all. I asked to see the first two scenes again.

"What can you tell us?" said the judge.

"The object of the exercise is to overtake. One of the recognised ways of doing that is braking later as you approach a corner. If, as here, you have a smaller lighter car, you can brake later, go up the inside and be past the car you have overtaken before the overtaken car has to turn into the corner. The ideal is for the manoeuvre to be complete before the overtaken car has to take the bend. What often happens is that the overtake has not been completed before the overtaken car has to turn into the bend.

"This is where it gets a bit more difficult. If the car which is being overtaken is still ahead in theory it is his corner. He can turn in and take the bend. Except now there is a car in the way, to his left. If he has been using his mirrors he will know there is a car there, that it has been trying to overtake him, and that there is not much he can do about it. Either he can give way or take the bend at a wider radius so that there is now room for two. If he doesn't know that there is a car there he will turn into that car. It happens quite frequently.

What you normally end up with is two cars with minor damage and two angry drivers.

"The complicating factor here is the second Lotus. While it was perfectly fair for the first Lotus to think he could out brake the Cobra and get the manoeuvre finished before the corner starts, you can't say the same about the second Lotus. How he thought *both* of them would get past the AC before the corner is beyond me. I hope that I'm making sense."

"You are," said Her Honour. "Please continue."

"I'm a lawyer, like you. I'm also an amateur racing driver. But I'm not a physicist. What I can't help the court with is whether the presence of the second Lotus helped cause the first two cars to flip over. What I can say though, is that putting his car there made a collision much more likely. Normally that is all there is – damaged paint, maybe a car so damaged it can't carry on with the race. But not this sort of accident. This is, in my experience, very unusual."

"Thank you, Monsieur," she said. "I will ask if my colleagues have any questions."

The middle avocat put her hand up. "Was the driver you went to help conscious when you got to his car?"

"No," I replied. "He was unconscious. I didn't want to move him because I'm not a paramedic, but then his car caught fire. I tried to put it out, but my extinguisher ran out before I could get the fire out. I decided I had to move him, and was in the process of doing that when the three marshals arrived and took over."

"What state was he in?" she asked.

"The roll cage had been pushed down onto where his head would normally be. I could see dish marks on his crash helmet. And he had a cut to the neck. There was blood on the top of his overalls. It looked bad."

"I'm sure that you did what you could. Thank you," she said.

No one else had any questions.

"Monsieur Westerfeld," the judge said, "we are very grateful to you for the time you have taken today and also very grateful for the efforts that you made to help Monsieur Smith. We are much in your debt."

"Not really," I said. "The poor man still died."

11

The last meeting of the year for which my car was entered was the late autumn meeting at Castle Combe. A relatively recent addition to the calendar, it was always well attended, not least because it was the nearest circuit for all petrolheads living in the far south west. For the two-day meeting, I was entered into the saloon car race on Sunday, a conventional fifteen lapper. It had not been touched since our return from Spa, but I was confident that an oil change, a change of brake pads and shoes, and some new tyres would be enough to allow me to run, without the need to trouble Terry. The fact that the rear axle ratio was taller than ideal, I would just have to put up with.

So, I was up early and at my parents' place in time for a late breakfast. My mother fussed more than usual about my health and welfare, and I was given something of a grilling about whether the police had caught the people responsible for running me down and damaging my house. Err, no. The bruising had faded to interesting shades of purple, and even my ribs had stopped aching. After bacon and eggs I pulled on my old overalls, jacked the car onto axle stands and started the engine with a view to warming up the oil so it would drain from the car better. Oil change accomplished I tackled the brakes. Changing front brake pads is straightforward, the rear shoes, slightly less so. The tyres were shot, but I had rung ahead and the supplier of the control tyre we had to run, a

Dunlop racer of a design identical to that run in the 1960s, would be at the circuit for the whole weekend. If I got to the track before the last race today, then I could bag my place in the paddock, sort the tyres out and potter over to the nearby pub where I was staying in time for supper. Scrutineering tomorrow morning was at 8.30am, with practice in the first session at 9.15am. So, with the car on the trailer, and all the associated kit loaded, I was on my way to Wiltshire by late morning. The M25 was, as usual, a bit sticky, but the M4 was clear, and I reached Chippenham in just over three hours. The rest of the afternoon was spent dealing with the car, chatting to other drivers and, to my considerable surprise, being interviewed by the race reporter of Motor Sport magazine, Simon Arron, who was running a series of profiles on typical classic car racers.

Word of our adventures at Spa evidently had leaked out. I was asked detailed questions about the Jeremy Smith incident, and I told him what I had told the court in Verviers. I also added my tuppence worth to the growing debate about driver standards, something gliding up the collective agenda as the sport of racing classic cars became more and more popular. Part of the difficulty is that the demographic of the drivers had changed. In the 1980s the entrants were usually the owners, and while you had to have some cash behind you to own and run, say, a 1950s 250F Maserati grand prix car, those who did were enthusiasts first and wealthy second. In the main they knew how to drive. More recently, owners tended to be successful businessmen, who, having sold up, now had the time and money to devote to historic racing. The values of the cars had soared in recent years, but just because you were a Fangio obsessive and now had the funds to buy his car, it did not follow that you knew how to drive it. It also did not help that race fans watching on TV would be treated to the sight of the BTCC boys at best rubbing paint or, worse, punting each other off without obvious penalty and unsurprisingly took the view that that was how it was done. Driving standards were markedly lower and people were starting to get hurt as I was all too aware. Having offloaded that gripe and collected the wheels back from the tyre lorry, there was just enough time to catch the last race. As if to underline my point it was red flagged due to two cars colliding on the way in to the corner before the pits, Camp, and two more cars not far behind, who clearly had paid no heed to the yellow danger flags being waved furiously, had then run into the two stationary cars. A marshal had been badly hurt in the process. Those two should, if there was any justice, have their race licences confiscated.

Signing on (examination of one's race licence) started at 8am, and I was near the front of the queue. Once that was done the next stage was scrutineering. That involves a detailed examination of the car, and race clobber, i.e., flame proofs, helmet etc. As we were the first scheduled practice session, being at the head of that queue was also important. The weather was a typical autumn day: bright sunshine, cold and damp. It was going to be slippery. Castle Combe is one of the circuits that sprang up after the war, having been an airbase during it. The track was the old perimeter road, much like Goodwood or Silverstone. Both of those places had been developed, Silverstone as a modern facility capable of containing Formula One cars. Goodwood had become the showcase for historic racing, but had nevertheless absorbed much investment. Castle Combe, privately owned, and out on a limb both figuratively and geographically, still imbued something of the spirit of the 1960s. Basic paddock, greasy spoon café, spartan pits and a fast and entertaining layout. It had acquired two chicanes in 1999, but that had not really diluted the feel of the place. It was still bloody quick and possessor one of the great driving challenges in the UK: Quarry. From the start line, going clockwise, it runs slightly uphill, through a quick right hander and into a flat left. A bit like Eau Rouge at Spa, though you cannot take it flat, or anywhere close to it, because it is immediately followed by a sharp, tightening, right hander with, just to add to the challenge, limited run-off. Wider than a hairpin, but slower than it looks, many optimists have run out of talent here, or real estate, and at best have slid down the grass on the outside of the track, or at worst clattered the barrier.

I had no desire to add my name to the list of victims, so as we filed out I was circumspect to the point of cowardice. The field was near capacity but a bit of a mixed bag. Some fifties saloon cars, including, I was pleased to see Freddie, Tolly's mate's grandson in his A35, some Mark II Jaguars, four Lotus Cortina's, numerous Anglia's and a couple of Mustangs. No Max De Vries. I was not sure if I was relieved or disappointed. A chat would have been interesting. Winning was unlikely, the podium possible. Practice was scheduled to last twenty minutes, so I couldn't feather-foot it for too long. I circulated for three laps, getting the temperatures right and doing my best to scrub in the tyres and brakes. New tyres and, in particular new brakes, could cause a terminal and expensive shortfall in stopping power just when it was most needed. What the car would have benefited from was a blast up the road the night before in order to bed in both, but it was no longer road-legal. I had no crew with me, so more by guesswork than anything else, I felt the times coming down. I had also to estimate when the session would end as my watch was buried under a pair of gloves and a Nomex suit. By the time of the chequered flag, there was a dry line on the track and I was getting into a nice rhythm. Not bad, but with more to come. The rest of the morning was spent catching up with friends, watching the rest of practice and ingesting an enormous fat git's breakfast.

Lunch was, officially, to last forty minutes after the end of practice, but with various delays due to recovering errant cars, no sooner than the last session had come in, we, as the first race, were being summoned to the assembly area. As usual, I was beset by nerves. One of the Mini Cooper exponents wanted to chat about Spa at that moment, and while I managed to resist the temptation to be sick on him, I could not talk and just walked away. I hated the hollow feeling inside, but I also knew that it was essential. I walked to the end of the assembly area and gazed across the track, trying to visualise the correct lines through each corner. I was put out of my misery by a piercing whistle: time to saddle up. Into the car, belts done up then balaclava, then helmet and finally gloves. The pack drove slowly round the track and we formed up in qualifying order, with me a gratifying fifth. Third row. Ahead were two Mustangs and two Lotus Cortina's, while next to me was a Jaguar.

At the five second board I selected first gear, let the revs rise to 4500rpm and watched the lights like a hawk. As they went green, I let in the clutch and the car lurched forward. For some reason though, progress was not maintained and the field poured past me as the engine bogged down. As I approached Quarry for the first time I was, I thought, about twelfth. I out-braked an Anglia on the way in, out-accelerated an A35 on the way out and as we approached the first chicane, I got past a further two cars. This put me into a bit of space so I concentrated on getting the next two corners right, including a small drift through Tower and sized up the gaggle of cars ahead. Two I managed to chase down on the way into the second chicane and got past them on the way out, and two I out-braked on the way into Camp, the right hander just before the pits. That put me into more space, so no excuses if I cocked up Quarry this time. Keep left through Avon Rise, clip the left apex neatly, hard onto the brakes on the way in, which unsettled the car, and then use the loose handling to your advantage to steer it on the throttle on the way through, nabbing the slide on the way out. *Very* satisfying. What was even more satisfying was finding one of the other Lotus Cortina's getting back onto the track having gone gardening. That meant, as best I could tell, three cars ahead of me. Two I could see entering the first chicane and I had a glimpse of one leaving it. Time to channel my inner Jim Clark. So, brake late, unstick the back of the car, try to put the inside front wheel over the kerb, and hold the drift as the car washes outwards on exit. Old Paddock and Tower were pretty text book, but I made a proper balls of the second chicane, having arrived far too quickly and ended up spinning onto the infield. Worse, as I tobogganed across the grass, a marshal's post that had looked reassuringly distant from the edge of the tarmac, started to come towards me at alarming speed. The car stopped just in front of it, engine dead.

Bollocks.

It fired, eventually, but all the good work of the last two laps was undone as all the cars I had passed came by, together with a couple more that I had to give way to before I could re-join. The last of which was young Freddie. He was still far enough ahead as we came up to the last corner for me to watch his line. He stayed off the kerbs, a good idea in an A35, as they do not require much encouragement to roll, got it turned in nicely and drifted gently through the corner with the car nice and stable, held on the throttle.

Good lad, I thought, you are nearly ready for something with a bit more power. I was tempted to stay back and watch him attack Quarry, but as it was coming up to half distance I wanted to put things right. I powered past him as we passed the pits, got one of the Anglia's through the next gentle right hander and then lined up three cars who were approaching Quarry. At best this was going to be rude, and at worst I was going to be guilty of the sort of over ambition that I had seen on the CCTV at Spa. Too late now. The first two were no problem, I was clean past them before the corner. The next though, while he left the door open, was one of the other Lotus Cortina's, so I could hardly claim that I had a weight advantage or more power. What was more, I realised that he was the car I had passed while he re-joined the track here the previous lap, so I could hardly expect him to oblige me again. And taking him out was not an option either. By now, hard on the brakes, with the back of the car skittering about, and the inside two wheels on or over the kerb, I slid more than drove up the inside of him. If he hasn't seen me we're screwed, I thought. Whether he had, or whether he was being a bit cautious after last time, he hesitated before turning in. By then I had my nose in front, and half on the grass, and well sideways, I was past, although there cannot have been a cigarette paper between us as I hustled by. How naughty you are is often factored by whether you get caught. I could – *just* – legitimately claim this was a fair pass, though he was unlikely to be doing cartwheels about it. The exit of the bend was untidy but I made the pass stick and then concentrated on reeling in the others.

The next time I passed the pits I saw from a fellow competitor's pit board that we had three laps to go. It took until Camp on that lap to catch the next group, which included one of the Mark II Jaguars. With a 3.8 litre engine it had about 120 more horsepower, but it was much heavier. As we came up to the corner I was close enough behind to slipstream him, and as he braked on the approach, I popped out and posted one up the inside. Derek Jones had been racing for decades and had an excellent reputation, so I was pretty confident that he would know that I was there. This time I was not really chancing my arm, which was a bit of luck because most of the spectators and all the stewards were watching what I was up to. I made the pass before the corner, was pretty sideways on exit, to the point that Derek pulled alongside me as we headed off towards Quarry. I kept to the right side of the track, knowing that I would have the line when we got there. So it proved, and despite his superior power he was still behind when we went through the first chicane.

The last two laps saw me having a good dice with Derek and making little headway towards the next group up. The result at the flag was, it turned out, fifth. If I had not spun it, third or possibly even second would have been the result. Ho hum. No cigar today, but much fun had and both I and the car were in one piece. Given the adventures of the last six weeks, I would take that.

I stayed and watched most of the rest of the afternoon's programme, before putting the racer onto the trailer and heading back to Essex. Progress was sticky as the typical Sunday afternoon traffic headed east along the M4. I was back at the farm by 7.30pm, and had the car and trailer stowed by 8pm. Which meant that I was home by 9.45pm in time to do the necessary homework for tomorrow.

12

The following week I was in Woolwich Crown Court. Woolwich is an odd court, in the sense that it's partly the local court for the miscreants of the Plumstead area, and partly the number one terrorist court in England. It would be quite possible for Court 1 to be hosting the world's press and numerous household name silks, while the rest of the building deals with the usual drunken punch-ups, stabbings, drug deals and bicycle thefts. Strangely enough, I would not be going in to Court 1.

I had a firearms case, which was at least at the more interesting end of business as usual. The police had stopped a car containing three men; in the boot there was a sports holdall, and in the sports holdall there was a cotton bag, and in the cotton bag there was a small revolver and fifteen rounds of ammunition. The driver had pleaded guilty, the front seat passenger had legged it and was the subject of an outstanding arrest warrant, and the rear seat passenger had contested the case and lost. I was in charge of the rear seat passenger.

On arrival at court I was somewhat surprised to find that the driver was represented by Daphne Edwards, last seen giving Gladys a hard time. Most of us both prosecuted and defended and were happy to do whatever came in through the door, but Daphne was much-loved by the Flying Squad and almost never defended this sort of thing. It was money well spent, though – by the time she sat down, I wanted to put my arm round her client and give him a cup of tea.

We stopped for lunch, and I headed to the bar mess to inhale a sandwich.

"James?" It was Daphne. She'd clearly just come up from the cells, and had a strange expression.

"Hello, Daphers – join me for lunch?"

"Can't – I've got a solicitor breathing down my neck for an update. But I've just had the oddest conversation with my client. He asked if you were James Westerfeld, the James Westerfeld who lived in Hammersmith. I said yes, mostly because I was a bit surprised, and he said that you had really pissed off someone he said that he couldn't name, and that he was sorry about your windows." The ghost of a smile twitched across Daphne's face. "He actually did look miserable about it, if that helps."

"What?" My mind was blank with surprise. "I – what?"

"Well, my thoughts exactly. I asked him what on earth he was talking about, and he mumbled that he'd already said too much and asked to go back to his cell. What the hell have you got yourself mixed up in?"

"My front windows were all smashed in two weekends ago, twenty-four hours after I was nearly run over," I replied. "It was possible that the car incident was an accident, but when the windows were put in…well, it seems personal."

"Bloody hell."

"Quite. Look, could you do me a massive favour, if you have the time – could you go down and ask him again if he'll say who it is I've pissed off?"

"Yes, of course," she said. "Frankly, I want to know the answer as well."

But neither of us were wholly surprised when he refused to say another word.

-

Not long after I got home, Claire Akely rang. My efforts to spring Bill's body had been successful, and he was now in the care of the undertakers in King's Lynn. The funeral would be in a fortnight.

"Please come," she said. "It's going to be hell, and I need a rock."

"Of course," I replied. "Are you having just a funeral, or a memorial service, or what?"

"I can't face spinning this out any longer. We'll have a funeral with all welcome; then it's done."

"That makes complete sense," I said. "Let's talk about something else – are you still sending a car to Estoril?"

"Yes. Tolly and two of the gang are leaving about now with Timo's GT40," she replied. "They'll be gone for over a week."

"Why don't you go? It'd be a change of scenery for you, and you could see what it's all about," I said.

"I can't. It's term time, and I have the dogs…" She trailed off, clearly thinking. "God, but the idea of flying away from all this…"

"It might do you good," I said. "Just to have five minutes to breathe."

She paused for a second. "If I went, James – would you come too?"

There were a hundred reasons not to, starting with the fact that I had absolutely no business being there, and ending with the fact that if my still-bruised ribs were anything to go by, spending time with Claire Akely was a serious health risk.

"I don't see why not," I said. "It'll do us both some good."

-

Almost the second I put the phone down there was a knock at the door. It was DC Perkins.

"May I come in, sir?"

I stood aside and ushered him into my sitting room. "Would you like a drink? Tea, coffee?"

"This isn't a social call, sir. I'm on duty. I have reason to believe that you've not been entirely candid with me, and I don't take kindly to being messed about."

"What do you mean?" I asked.

"One of our other enquiries has a strand with a Sussex dimension. To that end I spent quite a lot of yesterday speaking to one PC O'Dwyer. I think you've come across him."

"Ah."

"During our conversation he happened to mention that he had spoken at length to a man on my patch who had had both been run over and had his windows broken. He went on to say that this person was involved in some amateur sleuthing, and what had happened might be connected to the death of a racing driver. How am I doing so far?"

I said nothing, feeling foolish.

"It did not require a deerstalker and a big pipe to work out that I have only one person in the Hammersmith area who has been run over and had his windows smashed. If you're able to inform Sussex police of what you know, do you think you could see your way clear to assisting the force that is *actually* conducting your enquiry? Then we might make some progress." He paused. "And frankly I'm astonished that a criminal barrister would be bloody stupid enough not to."

I sat down, and closed my eyes. He was right.

"When I was hit by the car, I had no reason to suppose it was anything other than an accident," I said, slowly. "But when my windows were put in, obviously that changed. I should have called you then."

"You should. Why the hell didn't you?"

I sighed. "The problem is – well, quite a lot of this is speculation. I'm not sure of the full picture, and half the time I think I'm imagining the whole thing."

"You aren't imagining those broken windows, mate," he said. He seemed to be thawing a little. "Why don't you let someone who investigates this crap for a living attempt to sort the wheat from the chaff?"

And I so I told him everything. When I was done, he sat back against the sofa.

"Well," he said, "that's one hell of a mess."

"You're telling me," I said.

"Alright," he said. "Let me have a look into this. But for God's sake, cut the Miss Marple shit."

"I like to think of myself as more of a Peter Wimsey," I said.

"And I like to think of you as breathing," he said. "My guvnor will not have a sense of humour about this if you turn up dead."

He got up to leave, and then paused. "Oh, I almost forgot." He handed me a piece of paper. "Your knight in shining taxi's details."

-

Business was a bit slow that week, but to cheer things up, I had date number three with Flora. She'd spent the previous weekend in Antibes on another friend of a friend's yacht.

"Who was in the party?" I asked.

"There were quite a few of us," she replied. "Me, Susan, a couple of boyfriends of ours. Luigi who owned the boat – oh, and one of the people I saw at Goodwood. Timo someone?"

"Timo Aristophanes?"

"Yes, that's him. Seemed all right to start with, but was he thick as thieves with Luigi and they kept going downstairs to one of the sitting rooms to talk business."

"Do you know what that business might be?"

"Officially no, I don't. But Susan's mate Jeff knows him through sailing regattas. Luigi started life in Naples, dirt poor; now, not yet fifty, he owns this knob-out yacht. There's no big company, no trips to the office. Not much in the way of employees. He's just very, very rich."

"Drugs, or the Mafia. But how," I wondered "does someone like that not get caught? Payoffs? Luck? He may be protected in Italy, but you were in France."

"Not my area," she replied. "But I was bloody uncomfortable over the weekend. Even if they ask, I won't be going back."

"You have some glamorous friends, though. I'm not sure that I can compete with that."

Flora smiled. "Glamour isn't everything," she said. "No-one on that yacht made me laugh. Don't count yourself out just yet."

13

"D'you think we have time for another glass?"

Claire looked over at me, the ghost of a smile at the corner of her mouth. "We can always neck it if we need to."

We were sitting in the lounge at Heathrow, already two drinks down. Claire was looking more like the woman I'd first met at Goodwood; she was wearing a pale blue sundress, and her white-blonde hair was pulled back from her face, exposing the sharp angles of her cheekbones. She was still ethereal, but there was some substance to her; she no longer seemed like she would drift through the furniture.

"I have a question for you, James Westerfeld," she said, as I poured the wine.

"Shoot," I said.

"Why did you want to be a barrister? You keep saying you don't make any money, and you seem to be in court all hours of the day, and you spend all your time listening to the worst bits of people's lives. What's the appeal?"

"Oh, isn't it obvious?" I said, my voice light. "I'm an incurable show-off. No other profession would let me swan about making speeches and declaiming things – apart from acting, I suppose, but I can never remember my lines."

Claire looked at me, her pale eyes narrowed slightly. "That's a very clever answer," she said.

"Thank you," I said.

"What's the real reason, though?"

I paused with my glass halfway to my lips, and looked at her.

"Why do you want to know?" I asked.

She shrugged, and took a sip of wine. "I'm curious," she said. "You don't make sense to me. You've been so kind, helping with the books and the business and everything, I just – I can't imagine you yelling 'objection!' at people and scaring witnesses. I wanted to know – to know why."

"Well, firstly, no-one in an English court yells 'objection!'," I said.

Claire frowned. "Really?"

"Really."

"What happens if you want to object to something?"

"You stand up and say 'M'lord, terribly sorry, but I was wondering if you also thought that counsel's last question was somewhat leading…'"

Claire stuck out her lower lip, and for a moment she looked exactly like her son had when his sister had beaten him at skittles. "That is very disappointing," she said. "But stop dodging the question."

I put my glass of wine down. I couldn't remember the last time someone had asked me such a personal question. But I found that I didn't mind.

"What I told you wasn't total hogwash," I said. "I really do like standing up in court making speeches. Most civil barristers don't get to go to court very often, and I can't imagine it. There's nothing like it, not even racing."

Claire nodded, but didn't interrupt.

"What I like about it is that it's exciting," I said. "Every day I wake up and anything could happen. Every time I stand up in court, there's a little bit of me that knows that it could all go completely wrong, and that makes every little bit of procedural bollocks interesting because there's just that little bit of tension. And the drama of it, the spectacle – the daft wigs and gowns and the judges in their robes, the bowing and nodding and all that – it's just…I love being in court. I love the feeling of doing something tricky and a bit risky and everyone watching me do it, and sometimes do it well. I could tell you that it's because I want to help people, but that would be bollocks. What I love is doing it."

Claire looked at me, and for a moment I thought I'd been too candid. But then she laughed.

"I'm beginning to think that all blokes are actually nuts," she said.

I laughed too. "Why?"

"Because what you've just said – that was how Bill used to talk about racing. It was how Matteo – my ex with the Ford Falcon – used to talk about it as well. I always thought I just had a type. But now I'm beginning to think it's all of you."

"You need to broaden your sample size," I said. "Go and talk to some accountants. Or some solicitors, they're mostly dull as paint. Men who do something in insurance. It's not my fault you spend most of your time with us nutters who love to drive too fast."

Claire sighed. "True," she said. "But all the same, I'm keeping an eye on Jake."

"If he's anything like his dad, that's probably a good idea," I said. "Come on, that's us – let's go and board."

-

The reception committee when we arrived was Tolly and Timo Aristophanes. I'd never really spoken to Timo, although we had talked a bit at the impromptu party at the end of the Spa Six Hours. He was dressed in a Ralph Lauren shirt, chinos and loafers, with a dark blue sweater slung over his shoulders: the uniform of the European rich. Although he was the client and Claire, in theory, at least, was looking after him, he insisted that he take us to a little bar that he knew in Lisbon. He had the details in his phone and directed Tolly there.

Within minutes we were round the best table in the house, glasses of delicious chilled Portuguese white wine in front of us together with a steady supply of tapas. Every few minutes the boss or his wife would come over to check there was nothing we needed. It was a very entertaining evening, all the more so for being so completely unexpected. Timo had even squared our late arrival with the hotel, so when we bimbled in at 1.30am the night porter was waiting for us.

Saturday morning dawned bright and clear, and after a swift breakfast we were on our way to the circuit by 8.30am. We glided past security and were installed in the William Akely Motor Sport hospitality suite by 8.50am. Tolly fired up the coffee machine while the mechanics performed last minute checks on the GT40. Timo was entered in the one-hour race which required a driver change. On this occasion he had elected to drive solo, but he still had to stop – rather than get out of the car, his crew had to ensure that the car was motionless for no less than one minute.

In the previous two practice sessions, he had managed, consecutively, third and second. Another GT40 driven by a German crew had pipped Timo by four tenths of a second. He had spent a good part of yesterday afternoon with the mechanics checking and rechecking the engine settings to ensure that the car was giving its best. At this level of the sport, the car was also weighed at each corner on pads that were, in effect, fancy bathroom scales, and there was much ongoing discussion about whether to stagger the tyre sizes, or at least, the tyre pressures. We didn't worry about this sort of thing racing a Lotus Cortina, I noted ruefully. Timo reckoned that one of the two German drivers was excellent but his mate less so, so taken together he had the measure of them.

At 9.20am Timo was in the car and headed off to the assembly area, while Tolly, Claire and I made our way to the pit wall. I had never driven Estoril and now studied the track map on back of the programme. Just under three miles long, it runs clockwise, features a long pit straight, a tightening right hander at the end of it which fed into a complex of corners, then it opens out a bit before more wiggly stuff ends in a long sweeping right hander which leads onto the pit straight. There are also elevation changes, albeit not on the scale seen at Spa.

As we waited for the cars to file out, I asked Claire how many races she had actually been to.

"Apart from the day I met Bill, this is only the fourth," she said. "I went to one Goodwood Revival, but to be honest it was mainly to go to the Ball."

I laughed. "Well at least it's not too hard to follow what's going on."

Further conversation was cut short by the cars motoring slowly down the pit lane, all blipping their throttles. Doing that in a GT40 makes the ground shake. Just over two minutes later three GT40s hoved into view in line astern. Timo was the third car, more or less hiding up the exhaust of the car in front. I was impressed with his reflexes. On the next pass he was in second, evidently trying to line up the Germans for a pass into turn one. It was a forty-five-minute session and for over half of it the two of them had a proper bunfight, which was fun to watch standing on the pit wall.

Eventually the German team peeled into the pits for them to swap drivers.

Tolly was crouched over the watches and Ted hung out the board. As Timo was comfortably quicker that the second German driver, but had just been shaded by the first, there was no point in continuing to thrash the car, so we showed him the "IN" board with ten minutes to go. As he came down the pit lane and switched off, Tolly explained why we had called him in. I could see from the nodding of his helmet that Timo agreed with the logic and undid his belts.

As I had not been a guest of William Akely Motor Sport before, I was unsure how much of what was on offer was normal or how much Tolly and the crew had made an effort to ensure that Claire – who was, after all the boss – was as comfortable as possible. Once we had the car back to the truck, Timo, Claire, Tolly and I moved inside for coffee. Out of the fridge also came some excellent choux buns.

"Did you want to ask anyone to join us for lunch, or go somewhere else?" Claire asked.

"No and no," Timo said. "I'm very happy staying here with you."

Lunch was taken outside in the neatly roped off area. Between them, Claire and Tolly had excelled themselves. The table, which in naked form would not have looked out of place at any campsite in Europe, was disguised by a white linen table cloth, neatly clipped to the sides. A vase appeared, complete with fresh flowers, then China plates and Habitat glasses. Instead of the sandwiches, scotch eggs and sausage rolls I had been expecting, we were offered a choice of Coronation Chicken or medallions of pork with green beans. As well as water, Tolly, not quite with a tea towel over his left arm, offered a choice of beers or a chilled Chablis. Jim and Ted, now minus overalls but with miraculously clean hands, joined us for what was a cheerful lunch party.

The pressure was off for the rest of the day, so Claire, Tolly and Timo savoured the moment. We had started to discuss pudding choices when an unexpected visitor arrived.

"Mr De Vries," Claire got to her feet. "It's so good to see you."

"And you, Mrs Akely." His expression was genial. "Timo."

"Join us!" Timo said, pulling out a chair. "We're having a very serious argument about choux buns."

He and Timo began to chat about their racing plans for next season. I had just begun to relax when, in a gap in the conversation, Claire asked him what he wanted them to do about the state of his car.

"Sort out the damage over the winter, and give it any maintenance it needs. I'm hoping to do another European season, including the HRDC series. It would be nice to be invited to Goodwood again."

Tolly offered him pudding, but Max got up and made his goodbyes, looking thoughtful. I was beginning to feel like an idiot. He seemed like a perfectly normal driver; concerned about his car, excited for Goodwood, planning the season to come. What was I basing my distrust on – a sharp reaction to a nosy question? If I'd been asked about a private argument by a complete stranger, I couldn't say I wouldn't have given the same response.

After lunch Claire and I walked round the circuit against the traffic and found an empty grandstand two thirds of the way round the last long corner. We watched the talented and not so talented, sitting, to start with, in companionable silence. She leaned her head onto my shoulder, and I could smell the lavender of her shampoo.

"Thank you for coming this weekend," she said, after a while. "Having you around – the weight of it all lightens a bit."

"Of course," I said. "And after seeing the effort you put into lunch, I could see that Timo was impressed."

I could hear Claire's smile more than see it. "Well, it's nice of you to say. He ought to be used to it by now. It's what we always do for the drivers. Clients. Most of them have become friends, at least to Bill."

"Have you broached with Timo what he is going to do in the future?" I asked.

"Part of the reason for coming this weekend was to see what's what – what I can bring to the business, what I can leave to Tolly and the boys. If we kept going – obviously with the children, I couldn't get to all the races. But I could get to some."

"Who builds your engines?" I asked.

"Bill did to start with, and he did the work on Max's Alfa," she replied. "Our V8s are now built by a chap on the south coast who has an associated engineering business developing the internals of the motors. The downside is it adds to the cost, although people like Timo can afford it. But on the upside, it is something that we can do without Bill." She sighed. "God, I feel disloyal just saying that."

"You have to be practical," I said. "Do you want the business to continue? If yes, how can you make that happen when the boss isn't an engineer? You need to know what you can farm out and what the staff can do. If an engine goes bang at the circuit, who does the overnight rebuilds?"

"It has only happened a couple of times, but Ted mainly. Bill said that he's an excellent race engine builder. We have a good team. All of them have asked me if we're going to carry on. If we are, they want to stay." She paused.

"I suppose what I need to decide is – do *I* want to carry on? If we do, I'm shooting in the dark. If we don't, I lose the house."

"In a funny way then, Timo is your bellwether," I said. "If he stays, it's a pretty important vote of confidence; other clients will notice. Take him to one side this afternoon and have a proper chat. If he decides to leave, fair enough – it would be a shame but understandable, and I hope that you would part as friends. If he says that he wants to stay then you keep going."

"Thank you, James." For a fraction of a second, she squeezed my hand. "You make everything so clear."

I smiled. "Be careful what you believe from a barrister." She laughed softly. "I would suggest this, though: Bill's driving was one of the main shop windows of the business. I'd think about recruiting a part-time, top-drawer racing driver so that Akely cars still look fast."

"What about you?" she asked.

"While I would love to get my hands on Timo's GT40, I think you've wildly overestimated my skills," I said. "Why not have Timo ask Wilhelm Groen if he would be interested? He's a German DTM driver."

"DTM?"

"Germany's version of the touring car series. I really rate Groen, but more importantly so does Timo – he wouldn't be allowed anywhere near his car if he didn't."

"There are so many things I don't know."

"Everyone starts off knowing nothing. You just need to take it one step at a time."

-

I had thought that we would eat in the hotel, but Timo, evidently happy with life, suggested that we went back to last night's bar as his guests. The four of us got a taxi there, enjoyed a fine dinner and quite a lot of port, and didn't make it back to the hotel until past midnight. Timo and Max were on the fifth floor, but Claire and I were on the twelfth, and so I walked her back to her room. She was clearly a little tipsy, and holding onto my arm quite tightly. This close I could feel the warmth of her skin, and smell the sweet lavender of her shampoo again.

We reached the door and turned to one another. Our eyes met, and there was a long moment where neither of us seemed to breathe. Part of her hair had fallen down from her bun, and I moved very carefully to tuck it behind her ear. She leaned into my palm where it brushed her cheek.

"Thank you," she said. Her voice was very quiet.

"Of course," I said.

There was a sudden slam of a door closing at the other end of the hall. We pulled apart, as if caught, and I knew that I had to leave.

"Goodnight, Claire," I said, and leaned down to kiss her forehead. "Sleep well."

She didn't say anything in return. She just turned, opened the door, and disappeared. I walked slowly back towards my room, still reeling from the feeling of her against me. Perhaps that was why I didn't notice them. As I dug in my pocket for my own room key, something crashed into the back of my head. For one dizzy moment I felt myself falling; and then everything went black.

14

When I look back at the next few hours of my life, all I seem to have are the vaguest of snippets. The noise of seagulls. Terrible nausea. The feeling of something moving under me, as if I were in a car. And deep cold. I was so, so cold.

Time became a luxury. I just drifted. Occasionally I half thought that I saw people, but it was more impression than memory. From time to time I thought I heard voices, but nothing or no one I recognised.

When I finally came to, I was lying down. My clothes had been changed, and there was a hood over my head, although it was loose enough at the bottom to let me see a little, including my own bare feet. I couldn't move my hands, but at first I couldn't work out why. I was in some sort of cage. Three sides were closed, made of some sort of rustic brick work, and the fourth was an iron gate, open to the air.

I drifted for a bit, and then looked some more. My hands, I now saw, were tied together with rope, which was attached to a thick chain which looped through a metal cable around my waist and then ran back to a ring set into the wall. My skin started to itch, but as I tried to move my hands to do something about it, my stomach went into spasm.

Why was I here? Where was I? Was I being left for dead, or would someone come with food and water?

I remembered, very dimly, something I had once read in a book: that in a crisis, you should see what you had to work with. Upsides: I was alive. Conscious. Capable of rational thought. I still had some strength, in that I could move my legs, and I was just about warm enough.

Downsides: I was in a cage. I didn't know where I was or why I was here. The cage was more or less open to the elements on one side, and I did not know how cold it would get at night. My hands were tied. I was hungry, thirsty, and in pain. My watch was gone, so I had no way to tell how long I'd been there. I was lying on a cold dirt floor. And I was alone.

I tried for a bit to free my hands, but all I managed to do was wrench my shoulder and make my wrists swell so that the rope started to cut into the skin. After a while I changed tack. If I rubbed the side of my head along the three feet of floor along which I was free to travel, I found that the gap at the bottom of the hood widened. Despite my left ear protesting, it was worth it. The gap kept widening. I got shakily to my knees, and then shook my head back as sharply as I could. The hood fell off. If my throat hadn't been sandpaper, I would have cheered.

Now that I could see, I took a second account of my surroundings. I seemed to be in some sort of hillside barn, probably used by sheep or cattle farmers. Judging by the size of the ring at the end of the chain, cattle. I shuffled over on my knees to look at the ring, only to see that it was actually two rings, one half set into the wall and the second interlinked with the first. Both were about an inch thick. A blowtorch would be detained for some time getting through them. I certainly wasn't going to.

The rope round my wrists was new, as was the metal hawser round my waist. Using the wall as a prop, I dragged myself to my feet. The marks I now saw round my ankles suggested that my feet had been bound at some point; whoever had delivered me here clearly thought that was now unnecessary. The ring was not quite in the corner of the back wall, so if I started with my right shoulder to the wall, I could walk four paces until my left shoulder hit the side wall. A stabbing pain shot down my left arm, and appeared to linger in the elbow area, fizzing with indignation.

I tried to swivel the cable tether so that the pressure in my left shoulder eased, but all I achieved was more stabbing pain, which dropped me involuntarily onto my knees.

The thought swum into my mind that I had been left here to die. While my absence would be missed, in the sense that Claire, Tolly and the others would raise the alarm, how would they go about finding me? I didn't even know whether I was still in Portugal. I could see a patch of sky, and a bit of grass and some mud at ground level. The light was getting yellower. Afternoon, I thought. Dusk soon.

Almost all at once the sun dropped out of the sky and it was darkness. I was not the most widely travelled person, but I had read somewhere that daylight to dusk to darkness only happened like that near the Equator. Maybe I was in Africa? I knew that it was easy to be fooled by the heat of the day in Africa – it could get very cold at night. It was as if a switch had been turned off; my barn, having been tolerably warm, was now a very effective fridge. I started shivering. I couldn't make it stop and it made the whole left-sided ache even worse. I tried pacing for a bit, but I stopped being able to feel my feet and started stumbling. I sat down, back to the wall, beaten.

I must have fallen asleep for a while, because the next thing I was aware of was being colder than I have ever been. I was shivering so badly it almost hurt, and I couldn't feel my lower legs, hands or nose. I gritted my teeth and settled in to wait for dawn.

Without proper clothing or food or drink, I estimated that I had another day before unconsciousness took over. But until it came, I was going to do everything I could. I got to my feet, with real difficulty this time, and started to pace back and forth. I needed to get the blood flowing as best I could. It clearly had some effect because my feet and hands started to hurt like they had been plunged into fire. *Frostbite*, I thought. *Oh, God*.

Time passed. I watched the light start from the left of the gate and move round to the centre; if I was still north of the equator, I was facing south. To distract myself from the cold, I had another go at seeing how my hands were bound. The rope was tied in an elaborate figure of eight around both wrists. I couldn't see exactly how it was secured to the cable, but I could feel the metal strands. Try as I might, I couldn't get either hand free. All I was doing was making my wrists swell, and cutting the already dodgy circulation to my hands.

All too soon the light started to fade and the temperature dropped. I lay, too weak to pace now, thinking of all the things I had managed to achieve in my life, and a longer list of the things I hadn't. I hoped that I would be found, so at least my family would have some closure. I didn't think I would survive another night of the cold, but I curled up as tightly as I could and tried to surrender to sleep. I slipped into the blackness, and dreamt of deckchairs, and sunshine, and racing an Alfetta 159 at Goodwood.

I was in second place, giving a particularly well-driven ERA a hard time, managing the central throttle pedal and generally adding to the gaiety of the nation, when the intercom in my helmet burst into life.

"Shit a brick, mate, have we had a bugger of a job finding you!"

It was, unmistakeably, an Australian accent. I wished it away and carried on braking hard, changing down for the chicane.

"He's in here, Doug," the voice continued, "Out cold. Poor bastard is looking pretty shit."

As I powered the car past the pits, I felt a rough hand on my shoulder shaking me. "James. James. Wake up. We've found you. You're going to be OK."

"Who are you?" I mumbled, but it didn't come out.

"Give me the bolt cutters, Doug, will you? And some light."

A torch shone at my face at what seemed like impossible intensity, and I screwed my eyes shut as hard as I could. I felt him pull at my hands.

"Give us the knife, mate."

There was the sound of sawing, and suddenly my hands were free. He put down what was in his hand and started rubbing the circulation back into mine; pretty successfully, as the pain roared back in. He quickly dealt with the cable round my waist.

"Right, James. Can you stand?"

"I don't know," I whispered. "How long have I been here?"

"No idea, mate," he replied. "But you were kidnapped two days ago."

Two days ago? "Where am I?"

"Morocco. In the hills outside Marrakesh."

"Morocco? But I was in Portugal…" My vision was starting to blur again.

"Save it, mate," he said. "Can you walk?"

Two strong arms pulled me to my feet, but I was long beyond being able to stand. The men each took one side and dragged me out of my prison, towards the unmistakeable shape of a Land Rover. A rear door opened, and I was lifted onto the back seat, with one of the men sitting next to me to prevent me sliding onto the floor.

"Thank you," I whispered. "Who are you?"

The other man, who was now behind the wheel, turned to look at me.

"My name's Todd. We work for an agency that, among other things, finds kidnapped people. Now shut up and let me get you out of here."

The Land Rover coughed into life and we bumped for some time across broken land before hitting a rutted track, which in turn led to a road. My vision faded in and out, and after a while I closed my eyes.

The next thing I felt was the car drawing to a halt. A door opened, letting out a shaft of light and two nurses, recognisable by their clothing, pushed a trolley into view. Between them they lifted me onto the trolley and wheeled it inside. The lights seemed very bright as we rolled along a corridor. The foot of the trolley bashed into double doors which swung open to reveal a room with a bed in the middle of it. I was lifted again, and collapsed backwards. I tried as hard as I could to stay awake, but it was too much. The darkness overwhelmed me, and I was gone.

-

When I next woke up, I felt both considerably better and a hell of a lot worse. The feeling had returned to all my extremities, but as the majority of that feeling was pain, I was less grateful than I could have been. While I'd been out someone had hooked me up to an IV, and I suspected, from the slight cloudiness at the back of my head, that I was on at least a fair amount of painkillers. What the pain would be like without them was a grim thought.

I managed to pull myself a little more upright, and looked at my surroundings. It was a mostly empty room in what looked like a warehouse; the only things in it were my hospital bed, an array of beeping equipment, and a single chair. Sitting in the chair was a woman in scrubs and a hijab, working on what looked to me like a book of crossword puzzles. As I moved, she looked up.

"Good morning Mr Westerfeld," she said. "How are you feeling?"

"Better," I said. "But also, terrible."

"That sounds about right," she said, folding over the corner of her book. "Let me check your vitals."

"What – what am I doing here? What is this place? Why are you – who are you?"

"All in good time, Mr Westerfeld." She looked back over from the nearest machine. "Are you in any pain?"

"Yes," I said. "But I – what – "

"All in good time." She removed a syringe from a drawer and plunged it smoothly into the connection on the IV. "There, that ought to help. I can tell you a bit about how you're doing, if you'd like."

"Sure," I said. "Badly, I presume."

She shrugged. "Could be worse. You've been injected on a number of occasions in the neck with an opiate, probably diamorphine; when you arrived you were in withdrawal, which would explain why you've taken so well to the painkillers. You were severely dehydrated, hypothermic, and beginning to starve. Your ankles and wrists were bound tightly, but we're pleased to see the circulation seems to have come back."

I blinked. "It sounds like I ought to be dead."

"You probably should," she said. "But you're not, and we're intending to keep it that way."

"Good to know," I said, faintly.

She smiled. "I'll send Mr Mustapha in now."

"Who – "

But she was already walking away.

For the next twenty minutes I lay still, assessing the extent of my pain. It was slowly fading from my hands and feet, for which I quietly thanked every god who would listen.

The door opened, and a tall, thin man in a very good suit walked in. He had dark hair and a short dark beard, and very dark eyes behind expensive horn-rimmed glasses.

"Hello, Mr Westerfeld," he said, taking the unoccupied seat.

"Mr Mustapha, I presume."

He smiled. "Quite so. How are you feeling?"

"Like I would really, really like to know what's going on," I said.

"Well, that seems fair," he said. "Shall I start from the beginning?"

"Please."

"You were kidnapped in the early hours of the morning of Sunday 20th October," Mustapha said. "We weren't informed until lunchtime that day, and didn't get to Portugal until the evening; by then the local police were making enquiries. Mrs Akely was very distressed, and kept saying that it was her fault that you had been taken because she had suggested that you accompany her for the weekend. We had a lead on where you had been taken by dawn the following day."

"How?"

"Your captors made a useful mistake. When you were taken you had your mobile phone in your trouser pocket, yes?" I nodded. "They took it from you, but left it switched on. If you know how to do it and where to look, you can track that. By then your captors appeared to be moving south on a boat, about half way between Faro and Rabat, so we knew that Morocco was your likely destination. At that stage all we had to do was watch the scanner. Unfortunately, after you arrived in Morocco, either your captors realised their mistake or your phone battery ran out."

"Morocco isn't much to go on," I said. "How could you possibly narrow the search down to a small barn in the middle of nowhere?"

"Well, I don't mind saying it was quite difficult," Mustapha said. "We got lucky, as well. But we're professionals, Mr Westerfeld. Finding people is my business, and I am very, very good at it."

I looked at him, this quiet-looking man in his well-cut suit and scholarly spectacles, and felt a chill run through me.

"I'm not important," I said. "I'm not famous, or rich, or anything. Was there a ransom?"

Mustapha shook his head. "There was no ransom demand. At all. It looks as if your captors simply wanted you to disappear."

"Then – I mean, why wasn't I tipped over the side of the boat into the Atlantic?"

"My guess is that your fate hadn't been decided at that point," he replied. "But it's a good question. Keeping you alive really was a very reckless choice."

I looked at him again. "Who are you, exactly?" I asked.

"We are an agency," Mustapha said. "We are funded… discreetly…by a selection of government agencies and wealthy individuals. Don't concern yourself with the cost of your rescue. It's all been taken care of."

"And I imagine asking 'by whom' isn't going to get me very far?" Mustapha just smiled. "Alright, then – who went to all this trouble to get rid of me?"

"Ah." Mustapha frowned slightly. "That, I'm afraid, I don't know."

"I'm just a junior barrister," I said. "I don't – I represent shoplifters. Little old ladies who want to dodge their council tax. The worst I ever get is the odd murder, and none of them have two-pound coins to rub together. Why on earth would anyone want to kill me?"

"Not a question we can answer," Mustapha said. "I'm sorry, Mr Westerfeld. I can tell you that a boat trip from Portugal to Morocco is a standard drug-run journey. It would make sense to suspect that whoever took you was using the resources he had to hand; by that logic you're looking at someone in the drugs business." He moved his head from side to side equivocally. "But that's a guess. I'm sorry I can't be more helpful."

"You seem to have saved my life," I said. "I think that's probably helpful enough."

Mustapha got to his feet. "We contacted your family as soon as we found you," he said. "They are no doubt anxious to have you returned to them. We've booked you a seat on the BA flight to Heathrow that leaves tomorrow."

"Let me pay for that, at least," I said.

Mustapha's eyes crinkled. "I hope you don't mind me saying, Mr Westerfeld, that a single flight to England is not the kind of expense we worry about."

I closed my eyes. "Last question, then." I swallowed. "Am I still in danger?"

Mustapha looked straight at me. "Yes, Mr Westerfeld," he said. "We will be keeping an eye on you, but we can't be everywhere. Until we find out who it is that wants you dead, I'm sorry to say that you are in a very great deal of danger."

15

If there's one thing to be said for being kidnapped, it's that you don't have to pay for your own drinks.

I hadn't told anyone where I'd been, and the clerks had put it about that I'd been ill. This of course meant that every barrister in the Temple had heard about it by the end of my first week back, and every single one of them wanted the details over a pint.

To be honest, the clerks were kind; my first week back was mostly spent drinking tea and fending off questions from my roommate. By the end of the second week though, I was more or less back to normal.

I'd just got in on Wednesday night when there was a knock at the door. Once again it was DC Perkins.

"I had a conversation with an Australian this morning," he said.

"Ah," I said.

"Quite." I stepped back, and he followed me into the sitting room. "It seems you've had an interesting couple of months."

The story took a while. Halfway through, I went and got us both a beer. When I was finished, I got us two more.

"You certainly are making my life more interesting," Perkins said. "Alright. Is there anywhere else you can stay? It seems like they know where you live."

"I could stay at my parents for a while," I said. "But I can't hide forever."

He got to his feet. "You won't have to," he said. "We'll get them."

-

The following morning, I drove to Essex. The welcome was warm, my mother's cooking excellent, and the forensic cross examination much lighter than I had expected; I think both of my parents were a little shaken to be honest. I told them what I knew and spent much of the next few days either reading the paper or building up my strength by taking Bumble for walks. Physical fitness would not be a bar to standing up all day and talking bollocks, the definition of the job given to me by a client when I was in pupillage.

On Saturday morning I left my parents and drove to Claire's. As the Senator rolled to a halt, the kitchen door burst open and the dogs charged into the yard. Claire ran after them, and I was barely out of the car before she had flung herself into my arms.

"You're alright, you're alright." She was holding me so tightly I could barely breathe. "Oh, God, James, I've barely slept. I'm so, so sorry."

"Claire." I stroked her back. "Stop it, will you? *You* haven't done anything."

"I'm sorry," she replied. "Everything I have anything to do with seems to go wrong at the moment."

I laughed gently, and took a step back. "But I'm fine. Apart from some ugly marks on my wrists, I'm right as rain. Come on, let's go in – I think we could both use a drink."

Over a glass of white she filled me in on what had happened after I was taken. The morning after I'd been taken, she, Tolly and Timo waited at reception for more than an hour for me to come down. Eventually she went up to my room to find the door ajar, my case on the bed, and no sign of me. Alarmed, she told the others, and the hotel called the police. "And then there was nothing," she said. "Tolly made me see that I had to come back to England, to be with the kids, but, James, I thought – I thought you were dead, and…"

The composure she'd managed to gather up fell away all at once. We'd been sitting across from each other, either side of the kitchen island, but now I ducked around and wrapped my arms around her shoulders. She leaned against me, and I could feel her fighting to keep from crying.

"Shh," I said. "It's alright. I'm right here. Hale and hearty and ready to go and annoy some criminals tomorrow morning. There's nothing to worry about."

"Apart from the fact that someone *kidnapped* you, you great fucking *doofus*," Claire said, her voice muffled by my shirt.

I couldn't help it; I burst out laughing. Claire looked up at me, the beginnings of a smile on her own face, and then we were both laughing, clinging to each other, overwhelmed and relieved and for the moment, safe in each other's arms.

Our laughter slowed, and then we were just looking at each, still tangled together, Claire's face tilted up slightly to meet my eyes.

"James…"

I paused, my hand on her cheek. We were back in the hallway in Portugal; time slowed just the same way. But this time, there was nothing to stop us, nothing to interrupt the thought as I leaned in to –

"Mummy!"

It was Eleanor. By the time she rounded the corner of the kitchen, Claire and I were on opposite sides of the kitchen island again, both a little out of breath.

"What is it, sweetheart?"

Claire crouched down to Eleanor's level, and looked at the worksheet her daughter was clutching.

"Oh, I hated verbs too," she said. "What a tricky language French is, hey?"

"I've never got the hang of it," I said.

Eleanor looked up at me, seeming to realise I was in the room for the first time. "Oh, hello, Mr Westerfeld," she said. "What are you doing here?"

"Eleanor, darling, that's not very nice manners," Claire said.

"Sorry," Eleanor said.

"It's alright, Eleanor," I said. "I was just popping in to say hi to your mum. I had a bit of trouble getting back from Portugal, and I wanted to let her know I was OK."

"Was your flight cancelled?" Eleanor asked. "Our flight was cancelled once. We had to eat Toblerone for dinner because everything in the airport was closed, and then Dad fell asleep on the floor." Her face fell a little, and in that moment she looked so much like Claire it hurt.

"Something like that," I said. "Anyway, I'm back safe now, and I'll need to get going – I have court tomorrow."

"Where you wear the wig?" She and Jake had been fascinated by this detail when I first met them.

"Where I wear the wig," I said. "So, I'll be getting out of your hair."

"Sweetheart, stay here and rub out all of the bits you didn't understand," Claire said. "I'll walk Mr Westerfeld out to his car."

"OK, mum," Eleanor said. "It was very nice to see you, Mr Westerfeld."

"It was very nice to see you too, Eleanor."

We walked out into the gloom of the evening. From this angle, the lights above the island lit up the kitchen like a lantern. I could still see Eleanor very clearly, head bent over her work. I turned back to Claire.

"Claire…"

"I know," Claire said. "But – they're so young, James. And it's all been so recently, and – "

"Of course." I straightened up. "I'm sorry."

"I'm sorry too," Claire said. "I can't – James, I can't tell you how much..."

"Me too," I said. "But you're right."

We stood there, just looking at each other for a long moment. Even in the shadow of the house she was beautiful. I ached to move towards her. But I knew what the right thing to do was. And so I took one last look, and then nodded, and got into my car, and drove all the way back to London, very, very carefully.

16

I suppose that all unhappy marriages must start hopefully. But by the time they got to my desk, things were generally pretty bleak. This week's tragedy was a depressingly regular part of my workload: a grim domestic violence case. Over a five-year period Mr Bert Jenkins had bullied his wife Erica on a daily basis. He regularly slapped her, cut up her clothes, told her she was worthless, prevented her from seeing her family and on two previous occasions had assaulted her to the point that she had gone to the police. On both, she had withdrawn the allegations within twenty-four hours and they had gone nowhere. This time he had strangled her to the point of unconsciousness and not content with that, had broken her jaw.

So I was keen to get the bastard, to say the least.

I had checked in with the CPS and spotted that I had time to get a coffee before anyone else arrived. As I walked out of the court building and down the steps, two large men appeared.

"James Westerfeld?" the taller one asked.

"Yes," I said.

"I'm Detective Inspector Jarmel, and this is Detective Sergeant Draycott of the City of London Police. We have information that suggests that you are involved in the large-scale importation of class A controlled drugs."

I looked at them blankly. This was a bizarre joke to have pulled on a Monday morning.

"You are therefore under arrest for importing controlled drugs. You do not have to say anything, but it may harm your defence if you do not mention when questioned something you later rely on in court. Anything you do say may be given in evidence."

And then it hit me that they were serious. "I – I've done *what*?"

"Would you come with us, please, sir?"

From there things were a blur. Their car was parked on the pavement a few yards away and I was bundled into the back seat. We made rapid progress back to their base, which proved to be Snow Hill, next to Smithfield Market.

I was booked in by the custody sergeant and allowed a phone call. With as little detail as humanly possible, I explained to my clerk that he needed to contact Croydon Crown Court, and then my friend Sara Robinson, who was a criminal solicitor. Not that I didn't know the rules myself; but God knows two heads are better than one when the one in question is in the middle of panicking.

From the front desk I was taken to a cell. I had often wondered what it would be like to hear the door clang shut. Now I knew. Not great.

After a brief period of raw panic that my brain did not record very well, I tried to use the time until Sara arrived to work out what the hell the police had been told. Taking the decision to arrest such a member of the criminal bar in circumstances which would derail an ongoing trial was a big step. The police would have known that, so what they had, or thought they had, must be impressive.

Sara got there in just over an hour. I was released from the cell, and taken to a room where we could chat in confidence. The moment we were alone, she turned to me with an expression of complete shock, and then surged forwards and hugged me.

"What the fuck is going on, James?"

"I have no idea," I said.

"I mean – you? There are plenty of barristers I'd believe it of, but – you?"

I tried very hard for a weak smile. "Maybe I should be offended," I said. "Your estimation of me can't be that high if you don't think I could be running a secret drug ring without you noticing."

She stepped back, but kept her hand on my arm. "James, you could absolutely be running a secret drug ring," she said. "I just don't think you're enough of a masochist to keep taking shoplifting cases in Woolwich Mags if you didn't have to."

At that point a knock on the door produced the DS with the disclosure, and we settled down to read it.

The police had been tipped off that there was a tonne of heroin in a lock-up garage in Acton. The lock-up had been rented in my name. There was a statement from a letting agent of whom I had never heard stating that it was James Westerfeld who had rented the lock-up. My correct address had been given. He had been shown a photograph of me, originally taken of me leaving Lincoln Crown Court some years ago in a highish profile case, and was able to confirm that that was the man with whom he had dealt. And when the police cracked open the locks, there, in neatly stacked bundles, was enough heroin to cheer up an eighties metal band.

The police had next applied to the Crown Court for a disclosure order, so that they could check my bank accounts. My current account, which was usually hovering around a steady 'some money, maybe, if the clerks chased the Legal

Aid Board last month', was currently enjoying a heady balance of £230,000, almost all of it from three payments made in the last week.

The moment I'd seen the amount of heroin, my blood had run cold; when I saw my bank accounts, it froze altogether. If I was being fitted up, it was by someone who could afford to lose a tonne of heroin and £230,000 in cash to do so.

The DS left, and I gave Sara the quickest possible version of the past few months of my life. By the time we were ready for interview, Sara was looking at me as if I might actually have lost my marbles. In retrospect, I can't blame her. Being kidnapped and then rescued by forces unknown, possibly in connection to a series of motor racing accidents – it must have seemed considerably less likely than the possibility that I was an addict who'd gotten in way too deep and was now trying to cover it up. She'd had hundreds of clients like that. I knew, because so had I.

We all filed into the interview room, Inspector Jarmel, DS Draycott, Sara, and me, a stuffy little box in the bowels of Snow Hill nick. Despite everyone knowing that I could recite the rules in my sleep, we went through the standard preliminaries. Everyone introduced themselves. I was reminded that I was entitled to free legal advice, despite Sara's presence. I was cautioned. And then with all that out of the way, DI Jarmel laid out what they had.

"None of that happened," I said. It wasn't the strongest defence, but it had the advantage of being true. "I have no idea what's going on."

He slid a picture across the table. "This is the photograph, sir. Do you agree that that is you?"

I nodded. "Yes, that's me."

"Then why do you suppose he has made all this up?"

"As I say: I have no idea."

"The reality is, sir, that a man who is doing no more than conducting his normal business has identified you as the lessee of this garage. Which in turn links you to the substantial amount of drugs found in it. Or have I missed something?"

"He's lying," I said. In the dim, hazy part of the back of my mind which remembered that I was a lawyer, a thought occurred. "Can I see the rental agreement? It won't be in my handwriting."

He paused, looking momentarily troubled. "No," he said. "But if you provide a sample of your handwriting, we can have a look." I nodded. "Then let's turn to the other aspect: the payments of large amounts of money into your bank account. Is that untrue?"

"If that's what the bank say is in my account, then that's what is there. Do you have copies of my statements to hand?"

He raised an eyebrow. "I'm supposed to be the one asking the questions, sir."

Sara stepped in before I could answer him. "It's a perfectly reasonable request," she said. "It might, for example, show the source of the money. Do you have the bank statements or not?"

"No."

Another thought occurred to me. "Can you tell me when the payments were made?" I asked.

He rustled his notes. "The first was on Monday 4th November, in the sum of £87,000. The second was on Wednesday 6th November in the sum of £96,000 and the last was the following day in the sum of £47,000." These payments are consistent with involvement in the movement of high value narcotics and it is our belief that you are an international drug dealer." He looked triumphant.

"Well, if, as you say, I am an international drug dealer," I replied "with the means to turn £230,000 into at least four million at a stroke, I would be highly unlikely to be prosecuting a scumbag such as Mr Jenkins at Croydon Crown Court for the princely sum of nine hundred quid. For a start we would be discussing this in a location a lot warmer than Snow Hill Police Station. Further, someone has gone to a great deal of trouble to get me out of the way in the last month, and having not succeeded, it starts to look as if they are sparing no expense to ensure that this time they do manage it, ruining my reputation in the process."

Jarmel sat back in his chair. "I certainly would be interested to hear this," he said. "Go on then, Mr Westerfeld. Explain away."

And so I did. I told them the whole story, from the moment Bill Akely died to the moment they'd arrested me. Jarmel and Draycott had identical expressions, the pure, neutral listening face of policemen everywhere. When I was done, Draycott got quietly to his feet and left.

"That's a hell of a story, Mr Westerfeld," Jarmel said. "Do you have any evidence of this?"

"Well, you could check with the UK Border Agency who green lighted my arrival back into the UK on a document signed and stamped by a British diplomat at Marrakesh airport. I also suggest that you liaise with DC Perkins of Hammersmith Police who is investigating a possible attempt on my life and the smashing of all the front windows of my house. He has spoken to Todd Clark who works for the agency who found me. While they were not keen to reveal exactly who they were to me, no doubt they would respond to an official check. Someone has gone to much trouble to persuade you that I should be taken out of circulation, and you appear to have taken the bait. I completely see why you would think that, on the face of it, I am involved in the world of drugs, but there is a much bigger picture which I invite you to look for, see and act upon. Furthermore, while the banks have spent quite a bit of time, effort and money to ensure that fraudsters cannot take money out of an account, much less effort has been expended on stopping rogue payments *into* an account. If I had your bank details, I could pay any sum I chose into your current account. You would only be able to do something about it afterwards. If you had noticed."

He looked at me for long moments. "This interview is suspended." He got up and left without another word.

I was taken back to my cell. Time passed. Lots of it. Without anything to do, I tried to sleep, but I couldn't settle. The main problem was that every time I closed my eyes, I was back in that shed in Morocco; trapped, starving, slowly freezing to death. And when I opened them again, I was still trapped. The panic came in waves, hour after hour.

Just after night fell, the wicket in the door opened. It was an unfamiliar officer with a kind, round face.

"Ah, you're awake, sir. Would you like a cup of tea?"

"Oh God yes," I said. "I mean – yes. Yes, please. Milk and a sugar, please."

"Coming right up."

Within two minutes she brought me a steaming cup of tea. It helped immensely; the warmth of it, the sweetness. The concrete proof that even if I was trapped, at least this time my captors were people I understood.

Shortly after that, I and my tea were ushered into the private room for a chat with Sara. "You have really blind-sided them," she said. "I have known this custody sergeant for years. His youngest and my daughter were in the same class at primary school. They had authority to charge you and ask for a remand into custody. As a result of what you have said, Jarmel, who is a slippery bugger, has now got to do some actual investigating and he knows that what he finds is unlikely to help his case. It might take the rest of the night and into tomorrow, but my guess is you will be released on bail, with the condition that you surrender your passport."

"I haven't *got* a passport," I said. "I only have the stamped piece of card that got me home. They can have that if they like. Thank you. Am I going to be interviewed again?"

"I am told not. The desk sergeant has my mobile number so get them to ring me and I will come straight back. Unless you want me to stay, I think my work here is done."

"Go home, Sara. And thank you. It means the world to have a bit of moral support."

"Quite all right, love. I take it that I am appointed your solicitor? There's a sentence that I never thought I would say to you!"

"Yes, you are. I'll be fine. This is much more comfortable than school anyway. The tea is better. Go home and I'll call you when I get out. If I get out."

"You will," she said, and was gone.

-

I was held there until late afternoon of the following day. When I emerged from my cell, there was a different desk sergeant and DS Draycott, but no sign of Jarmel.

"You're being released on bail," Draycott said. "You're free to go. We talked to your friend DC Perkins," Draycott said. "As insane as your story is, he could confirm enough of it that we're willing to let you out for the minute."

Thank God for Perkins, I thought. *Thank God he wanted to know what happened next.*

"Thank you," I said. "I – thank you."

And so I was handed my shoe laces, brief case, mobile phone and wallet and shown to the door.

When I turned on the phone it was teeming with messages. My clerk was responsible for half a dozen of them, as was Laurence Anderson QC, my head of chambers. My stomach dropped. I knew what he was going to say.

The thought of having that conversation over the phone was more than I could bear at that moment. And so, somewhat dazed with exhaustion and the sweaty aftermath of raw terror, I walked out into the late afternoon sunshine and back to chambers.

When I was a first-year tenant, I got absolutely plastered at a Christmas party and did the Macarena on a pub table. The following morning, hungover and knackered, I had sat in the little café on Tudor Street and tried to work out how to get to my room in chambers without running into a single other person. Two coffees in, I'd figured out that if you used the side door which opened onto the Inner Temple gardens, you could sneak through the clerk's kitchen and up the back stairs. All these years later, the side door was still there. I slipped through, hurried past a junior clerk I barely recognised, and made it up to Laurence's office without seeing another soul.

I didn't know him that well. He had led me once, and we had co-defended in a case with him leading a colleague. He was smooth on the surface, but I had absolutely no illusions that he was anything other than completely ruthless when it came down to it.

"James," he said. "I wasn't expecting to see you."

"No, I imagine not," I said.

"Come in," he said. "And – well, I think a glass of whiskey might be in order, don't you?"

I considered declining; God knows I was already out of it. But instead I nodded, and he poured two very stiff ones from a beautiful crystal decanter.

"I don't think there's any point in beating around the bush here, James," he said, when I'd swallowed about half of the whiskey. "You must understand that I require your resignation from chambers."

"Well, you can have it if you still think such a course is merited when I have finished," I said.

"What the fuck do you expect me to do? I had the Resident Judge at Croydon on the phone for most of this morning, complaining that, a) your conduct had derailed a serious trial which involved a four-year-old giving evidence, and b) how was it that our chambers should be foolish enough to have an international drug smuggler?" He was clearly very angry.

"He seemed remarkably well informed," I said.

"Yes. In yesterday morning's post was an anonymous letter setting out what you have been up to. That is strange, I will grant you." Some of the heat went out of him.

"Someone has gone to a great deal of trouble and expense to make it look as if I am a drug dealer. I take it that you at least, was aware that I had been kidnapped?" I asked.

"Not the details, but yes," he replied.

"You need to hear the whole story." So, I told him. I was getting good at this.

When I had finished, he looked at me for quite a while. "Right. Judge Wood and I were in pupillage together. He is a mate. I will call him and fill him in on what is going on. You had better be telling me the truth, because I will ask him to pass the word that you have been stitched up. I apologise for my hostility earlier."

"This has all become a little wearing," I said. "What is going to happen next? Don't answer that. But the villains will be pissed off that I got out of Morocco, and, I imagine that with at least half a million down the tubes, boiling with rage that I am still out and about. Are they going to stop there? I doubt it."

"Hhmmm. Tricky, I agree," he replied. "The other problem is what are we going to do with you in the meantime? Officially you are under suspicion and on police bail. I'm not sure it is really on for you to prosecute any cases at the moment. The options, it seems to me are these: you are innocent until proven guilty, so you could carry on, defending only. You could retreat to your parents and ride it out there, or similarly with a friend, preferably out of London."

"I am a cussed bastard," I replied. "I *really* don't like being pushed around. I recognise that in the short-term prosecuting is not really an option. But if I go and hide out of London, it is like giving in to the IRA. They've won. I would rather stay, work as and when I can, operate from home and flick V signs at those who wish me ill. By the way, can you get Judge Wood to hand the letter he received about me to the police?"

He looked amused. "Good man. Yes, I'll tell him. I suggest that you speak to your bank manager, that is, if you still *have* a bank manager, and sort out what to do with the rogue payments. You need those out of your account as soon as. You will also need to make your peace with the Bar Standards Board. My guess is that you will be allowed to defend the existing work you have, but not take any new work. And be in no doubt that if you have lied to me, I will haunt you to the end of your days."

With that I took the Tube home, contemplating a life of near total unemployment.

17

Two days later I was woken from a late-afternoon nap by a hammering on my front door. I padded downstairs blearily, and was stunned to find the smiling face of Todd, my Australian rescuer.

"What on earth are you doing here?" I asked, beyond surprised.

"Mustapha sent me," he said. "We were informed of your recent adventures, and the decision has been taken to elevate the level of security. I'm it. Can I come in?"

"I – yes, of course." We moved to the kitchen. "Tea? Coffee?"

"Tea please. Builders, one sugar."

I made us both tea, and handed over to him.

"Ahh," he said, appreciatively. "Bloody airplane tea. However much you pay it's always shit." He looked me up and down. "You look crap, mate."

I looked down at myself. He wasn't wrong. I was in old pyjamas, with a coffee stain on one cuff, and I hadn't shaved since I'd been released. I hadn't done much of anything, really. After delivering my passport, or rather the stamped card, to the local nick, I'd gone back to bed, and more or less stayed there.

"Considering the last time you saw me, that's not great to hear," I said.

Todd laughed. "Good to see you're not completely braindead. Come on, show me to my room."

"Your room?" I nonetheless got to my feet.

"My bedroom," Todd said. "D'you think I can be a bodyguard from a hotel? I know you've got two spare rooms, so cough one up."

Somewhat dazed, I did.

"I've never had a bodyguard before," I said, and then realised how stupid I sounded. "How does it work?"

"I won't be painted to your side," he said. "You might be able to have a shit on your own. You'll tell me where you're going and how you plan to get there, and then I'll decide how close I need to be. You don't bullshit me." This evidently wasn't a request.

"No. Of course not." I stood back; he had thrown a kit bag onto the bed, and was stripping off his jacket. "I guess – welcome to the house?"

He grinned. "Lovely to be here." He looked up. "So? What's on the menu today?"

I scoured my brains for something sensible that needed doing, mostly so that it didn't seem like I'd been planning a day of sleeping and not thinking about anything. "I need to go to Croydon," I said. "To collect my wig and gown and my paperwork and all that."

"Alright then," Todd said. "Go and get changed, then. And for fuck's sake, have a shower first. I'll meet you back in the sitting room in half an hour."

And so I did as I was told. Honestly, at that point, anyone with a clear opinion would have persuaded me.

I was expecting us to take the Senator. Instead, when I stepped out of my front door I saw a Range Rover Sentinel sitting next to it, looking completely out of place.

"No point in taking chances," Todd said, cheerfully. "Besides, it's got cup holders."

"The dream," I said.

We drove slowly to Croydon, taking in the sights of Wandsworth, Tooting, Streatham, Norbury and Thornton Heath. At the court you can park outside for a limited period, so I left Todd in the car, took a deep breath and headed into the building.

The robing room was, for once, empty. I collected my things, which had been left in a tidy pile on one side of a table, and then took a look around. Being a barrister was the only thing I knew how to do. I was pierced suddenly with the terror of the thing. I might never practice again. The only life I had ever known might be over.

And then I did the English thing, which was to swallow the small sob in the back of my throat and get back to what I was doing.

-

We crawled home through the lunchtime traffic. I retreated to my study, a converted attic with a Velux window, and read a Patrick O'Brien novel for six hours straight. What else was there to do? I had no idea what Todd was doing, and frankly, I had run out of energy to wonder about it.

At seven, I wandered downstairs. To my surprise, my kitchen was full of the scents of grilling steak, recently opened wine, and cooking onions. Todd was wearing a frilly apron that an old girlfriend had left behind, carefully flipping the steaks.

"You looked like you haven't eaten for a bit," he said. "Sit down and tell me what you think of that red."

I obediently poured myself a glass and tried it. It was outstanding, and I said so. Todd grinned.

"You Poms don't know shit about wine, so that doesn't mean as much as it could, but it's a start. Drink up, mate."

For the next two hours, Todd explained, with very little interruption from me, that it was his dream to open a winery of his own back where he'd grown up in Hunter Valley in New South Wales. Before long I'd gone and got an atlas, and he held forth about terroir and why wine from Wollombi was the fucking tits. I didn't say much, but I ate what was put in front of me and drank what I was told to drink. That night I slept like a human person for the first time since the arrest.

Two days later, I arranged to go to the pub with Chris. Given the pub was yards from the end of my road, Todd agreed I could probably manage just fine without him for an evening, and so I headed off alone.

The best thing about Chris, as a friend, was that he was wholly uninterested in my personal life. In all the years we'd been friends, I still had no idea whether he was married, divorced, had children; I'm not sure he remembered that I was a barrister most of the time. We just loved to talk about cars. By the end of the first bottle, we were swapping plans for our dream garages; so somewhere down the second, I apparently, was going to have the cash to buy and run a 1951 Grand Prix Alfa Romeo 159. For a few hours, none of the rest of my life existed.

Chris headed home at eleven, and so I finished the bottle and then began to walk home. Just as I was leaving, Todd called.

"You alright, mate?"

"Absolutely fine," I said. "I'll be home in – "

But a dark car had pulled alongside me. As it stopped the back doors sprung open, and two very large men jumped out.

"Todd," I said. "I think I'm about to be kidnapped again." My voice was completely calm. At some point, I had crossed into acceptance.

I could hear him drop something. "Make as much noise as possible and do your utmost to struggle," he said. "Stall them."

The giant nearest me grabbed my arm.

"Leave me alone," I said at not much more than normal volume. To be honest, I don't think I'd ever shouted before. It felt almost rude. As he started to force my head into the car, I finally got the hang of it. "Help! *Help*!"

I did my best to struggle, but they were so much stronger than me. It was hopeless. I inhaled to give it one last go, when I heard a solid "whumph". The first giant let go of me. His partner was still trying to propel me into the car; and then he too suddenly fell away. As I straightened up I saw why: Todd had arrived, and had winded the first one, who was on his knees on the pavement trying to get his breath back. The second was bent over the boot of the car, looking unsteady.

Todd wasn't done. He'd turned his attention to the driver's door; he got it open and was starting to pull the driver out when he stamped on the accelerator and the car shot off, leaving the two men lying on the road.

"Fuck's sake." Todd knelt down, and within seconds had zip-ties around the wrists of both attackers. "I almost had the bastard."

I was in the process of attempting to make my phone work, but my hands were shaking so much I could barely open it. Thankfully one of the nearby householders must have called the police, because within moments two police cars screeched to a halt next to us.

A very long two hours later, we were driven home from the police station. We'd both given statements, although

I noticed that Todd's was almost entirely untrue; he lied so cheerfully and confidently, and with so many legitimate-looking bits of ID, that no-one batted an eyelid.

"I'm sorry, mate," Todd said, as we both sank into chairs at the kitchen table. "I underestimated the threat to you badly, there."

"You saved me," I said. "I'm not going to be complaining about the methods."

He smiled, somewhat weakly. "Still. No more unescorted trips to the pub. In fact, no more trips to the pub full stop."

I put my head down on the table. "Sounds about right," I said. "I was having far too much fun."

18

The next few weeks passed quietly. I read a lot of novels. I read the jobs section of the *Times*, and tried to imagine myself doing anything that wasn't criminal law. I went for runs with Todd, which was a humiliating experience; he could have beaten me running backwards in stilettos. I thought about Claire, and didn't call her. Todd taught me some basic self-defence, and then we drank beers in the garden while I iced whatever new selection of bruises he'd given me the day before. It wasn't the worst period of my life. But I was aware that I was drifting.

With Todd's approval, the first week in December brought Mr Bularenko's trial. The intervening months without alcohol had caused him to lose weight, appear less florid and talk a bit more sense than when I had seen him at the preliminary hearing. Since then, I had visited him in prison twice and organised leading counsel who would be doing much of the talking, Humphry Easter QC. I was looking forward to how he was going to smooth this over. A conviction for murder would be harsh, but the lesser offence of manslaughter seemed, at least to me, to be the most likely verdict. We were pushing for an acquittal, but keeping our expectations well under control. As part of the Defence preparations we had had the CCTV from the council enhanced with a view to seeing the knife in Mr Kowalski's hand. Without result.

We were before HHJ Hines. So a fair trial was guaranteed. As was an off-the-scale sentence if we lost. Watching Humphrey in full sail was to be given an advocacy lesson I would remain grateful for, for the rest of my career. If I still had one, that is. He was superb with the party-goers, conceding nothing, advancing our case all the time, and repeatedly but subtly ramming the point home that these people were getting heroically pissed in the garden of someone that they had never met. More than once, the simple question "Who invited you to the party?" was greeted with silence. An occasional variation was, "Why did you think you were welcome at that house?" Tricky if you did not know the proprietor. It was good sport and brilliantly done, but as the trial progressed and we talked the events of the day over in one of a number of Lincoln's excellent restaurants, even if the jury gave him the benefit of the doubt as to Kowalski having the knife, explaining a two-pace run-up together with a blow that would have stopped a hippopotamus as self-defence was not going to be easy. And of course, the level of alcohol consumption did not assist either. Apart from the two day lay-down prior to interview, the police, understandably anxious for him not to die on their watch, had called out a doctor and taken a blood sample. When analysed for alcohol consumption, he was found to have 395 milligrams of alcohol per 100 millilitres of blood, which made him a whisker under five times the legal limit, had he been driving. Happily his interview stood up well, so the Crown's case ended, from our perspective, on a high.

We started the Defence case at the beginning of week two. Mr Bularenko, dressed in a smart suit and with the occasional help from an interpreter gave a good, and surprisingly full account of the evening's events. At one point Humphrey asked him, "Given that you had drunk a very large amount over the course of that day, how much has that affected your memory?"

His response was, "We Ukrainians can take our drink. Not at all."

The jury actually laughed.

As Humphrey finished, Mr Bularenko volunteered this, looking straight at the jury, "Whatever you decide, I want you to know that this was the worst day of my life and there hasn't been a day since where I haven't wished that it had turned out different." It sounded as if it came straight from the heart.

The position got a bit stickier when the Prosecution QC stood up. Thomas Enright QC was not one of the Bar's shooting stars. Which is not to denigrate his effectiveness. After all the tortoise beat the hare. His approach, low key, but thorough, very thorough, gradually wore Mr Bularenko down. He spent a morning on what was going through his mind as he ran up to hit Mr Kowalski. Yes, he had been hit first. But had the amount that he had had to drink clouded his judgement at all? Couldn't he have walked away? Why was it necessary to take a run-up? And so on. All the while the picture of a more malign intention than Mr Bularenko was admitting was coming into focus. Sexy? No. Devastating overall? Yes. From the Defence point of view, while not reduced to a smoking ruin, our case had certainly been given the sort of stonking not seen since D Day.

The advocacy lesson continued with speeches. Enright's was unshowy as expected, but it was full of detail and gradually built to the conclusion that the only conceivable verdict consistent with the jurors' oaths and the evidence, was guilty of murder. No pressure then. Humphrey's approach was more upbeat, funny to the point that the jury laughed at what he said more than once. Our man had been struck first. He could not know what Kowalski was going to do next. These people had come to him, and at no point had he been the aggressor. He had had a split second to weigh up what to do in a pressure situation not of his making. I was pleased to see that the majority of the jury were making notes, some extensively. While not a guarantee, it did at least mean that what we were saying was being taken seriously.

Come the summing-up it was as expected. Scrupulously fair, he bent over backwards to ensure that the jury had all the points we had made on our client's behalf. This was potentially dangerous. The Great British Public are, in the main, fair. But it is a well-known national characteristic that we do not take kindly to being told what to do. There is an apocryphal story dating back to John Mortimer's days as a senior barrister at the Old Bailey. At the end of a murder trial, which concluded with an unexpected acquittal, the usher responsible for tidying up the courtroom before the next case found a note in the jury box. It read: "Do we all agree that the defendant is guilty? And that the judge is biased in favour of the Prosecution? So, therefore we acquit?" Telling, or worse, *ordering* a jury to convict was almost always counter-productive. However, rowing out the defendant in the summing up could have a similarly adverse effect, leading to an unexpected conviction. Which, in terms of sentence, the judge was bound to honour. And it was no use going to the Court of Appeal either, as they would merely point out benignly that the judge could not possibly have been more fair, leaving the result to stand. From what I could see, HHJ Hines remained on the right side of this, sometimes a hard to spot line, but you never knew. They retired to consider their verdict on Thursday morning.

Waiting for a jury was a task tackled by different people in different ways. Some beavered away on papers that had come in during the case. Others chatted and laughed about the imponderables of life. For some reason, impossible to fathom, the robing room at Lincoln was particularly conducive to the chatting and laughter. Once set up with coffees, Humphrey and Enright started telling increasingly funny war stories, some of which had happened to them and some concerning now long dead legends of the criminal bar. I missed the start of all this because I went down to the cells to see how the client had viewed the summing up. Humphrey, the solicitor and I had had a lengthy post mortem after he had finished his evidence. Overall, we all agreed that the trial had gone as well as could be expected. Managing the defendant's expectations was a key part of the job. Mr Bularenko knew that a verdict of guilty of manslaughter was on the cards. We both agreed that we could not ask for more from the judge. The day passed in a flash until the jury were sent home. That night we met up with Enright and his junior, and the four of us took the judge out to dinner.

Case dinners remain one of the nicer traditions of the English Bar. Few cases merit them, but something lengthy or serious enough would qualify. A murder certainly did. Such an event was normally better done after the whole case was concluded, whatever the result. However practical reasons here militated against that. If the verdict was returned on a Friday, everyone would be keen to get home for the weekend, so that didn't work. If the jury were still out into the following week, I would be holding the fort on my own as Humphrey was starting something at the Old Bailey. Enright too, had commitments elsewhere. In those circumstances I would be staying at William the farmer's, which made a case dinner awkward. So, on the strict understanding that we did not mention the case, and to ensure that we were all there, it was tonight. Having scouted out the best of Lincoln's restaurants, something Enright seemed to have a nose for, we picked one and enjoyed a very convivial, delicious dinner. All present knew that if HHJ Hines was required to sentence our man, for either murder or manslaughter, he would be utterly professional. And tough.

On the dot of 10am the jury were sent out to carry on their deliberations. I had another minor hearing in one of the other courts mid-morning, but like the previous day much of the morning was spent pretending to read the paper and listening to improbable accounts of what past titans got up to when faced with judges they did not like. It was mid-afternoon when we were tannoyed into Court 1. Verdict. My regular musings as to how a defendant felt at this moment in a murder trial was about to be demonstrated. Credit to Mr Bularenko, he had been told it was a verdict downstairs. He came up the steps, smiled at Humphrey and I, waved to his family and supporters in the public gallery behind the dock, and acted as if he was facing some minor parking misunderstanding rather than the possibility of spending the next fifteen to twenty years in prison. My insides were awash.

The jury filed in and sat in their same places. Another myth with just enough grounding in fact for it to have some traction, is that you can tell what the verdict is by their collective body language before they deliver it. The theory is that if they come in and beam at the dock, they will acquit. If they file in, and all stare at the floor, they will convict. The wheels come off this analysis with mixed verdicts, or ones that they know will upset one party or another. On this occasion they sat quietly and avoided looking at Mr B. Oh shit. "Will the Foreman please stand?" said the clerk. A male juror on the front row stood up. "Will you please answer my next question either yes or no. Have the jury reached verdicts upon which you are all agreed?"

"Yes," said the Foreman.

"On Count 1, do you find Andreas Yuri Bularenko guilty or not guilty of murder?" asked the clerk.

"Not guilty," said the Foreman.

"On Count 2, do you find Andreas Yuri Bularenko guilty or not guilty of manslaughter?" asked the clerk.

"Guilty," said the Foreman. He was then asked to sit down.

Enright was straight onto his feet telling His Honour about our client's few and minor brushes with the law. With that, Humphrey rose, slowly and deliberately. A hitherto unseen part of his armoury was his ability to change the timbre of his voice to something softer than usual, as a way of maximising the sympathy to be accorded to the defendant. On the upside this was not an incident of our client's making, set against which was the industrial quantity of alcohol consumed, although some leeway was to be given for the fact that this was something of a cultural or universal lifestyle choice in the circles that Mr Bularenko moved. And His Honour had heard the volunteered expression of remorse at the end of his examination in chief. It was sublime, and the Judge was nodding and looking pensive. When he had finished he rose and said that he wanted time to consider the proper sentence. This happens occasionally, with the unintended consequence of ramping the tension still further. We both knew, though, that we had done everything in our collective power for Mr Bularenko, and unless he veered outside the recognised sentencing guidelines we would be stuck with the result.

Twenty minutes later HHJ Hines was back in court. I had watched him sentence those he clearly took a dim view of on a number of occasions, so I knew from the tone of his voice that he was not without sympathy for our man. He went through the facts in outline, commented on the levels of drink taken and noted his relatively clean past.

"Stand up. Andreas Yuri Bularenko, you will have on your conscience until you die the fact that you have taken a life. It is impossible to know what your reaction would have been to Mr Kowalski had you been sober, but I view the amount of alcohol consumed as the prime aggravating feature in this case. I accept, though, that he was the aggressor, something implicit in the verdict of the jury. Taking all these factors into account, the least sentence I can pass in this case is one of four and a half years. You will serve half that sentence, and when released the sentence does not come to an end, for you will be on licence for the remainder of it. Take him." With that he vanished downstairs with the goalers.

Fifteen minutes later we were in the small interview room in the cells. Humphrey and I, the solicitor, Mr Bularenko, and the interpreter meant that there were not enough chairs. These days they were fixed to the floor, so simply moving them about was not an option. I stood. These post-match interviews can be sticky affairs. This one, however was anything but. Mr Bularenko cheerfully conceded that he was very happy with the manslaughter verdict and happier with the sentence. He had been very worried about being convicted of murder. He thanked us for our efforts, and assured us that he would be spending the next two years before release thinking about his lifestyle choices. He was so upbeat that anyone would think we had got him off.

Once back on ground level we offered Ron, the solicitor a drink, but he declined as he had to hot foot it to his son's school. Humphrey declined my offer of a lift to London on the ground that he had a lot of reading to do for next week which was better done on the train. He did, though, accept my offer of a lift to the station. Sometimes, just occasionally, things go your way in this job. It was a very acceptable result.

19

Come mid-January, I was sitting in my to study, trying for the third time to rewrite my CV, when I got a phone call from Michael Ferguson. I'd told him a little about what had happened, although I'd not gone into the details; God knows I didn't need yet another person thinking I'd lost it.

"Look," Michael said. "I know you're going through it, and I reckon you could use a change of scenery. Come and stay with me at the house here."

"In Antigua?" Michael had retired out there a few years back; apart from visiting his family and doing the racing season, he spent most of his time in the sunshine. "Really?"

"Really," Michael said. "It must be pissing it down in England this time of year, and I bet you're moping around with no work to do. Come and drink rum with me instead."

I opened my mouth to explain that I would have to run it past Todd, and then closed it again. *Let me check with my bodyguard* made me sound like a pillock.

"Come on, say yes," Michael said. "I've invited Claire Akely as well, it'll be a fun party."

My hand froze, halfway to scratching my nose. "Claire – Claire Akely?"

"You know, Bill's widow," Michael said. "Poor thing's had a rough time of it – I don't know her that well, but I went over for dinner at theirs once back in the day, and I thought – well, I thought she might like a break, to be honest."

Say no, I thought. *Say no, you can't. You're busy doing something else that's very important. Say no.*

"You know what, Michael," I said. "That sounds like a brilliant idea. I will need to replace my passport and get the permission of the court to go. As you know I am on bail."

"Well hurry up," he replied.

I was surprised when Todd told me he wouldn't be coming with me.

"Nah," he said. "We've got people out there already. I'll stay here, keep an eye on the house. Anyone tries to bust in while you're gone will have a traditional Australian welcome."

A successful trip to court and an urgent request to the Passport Office later, I was on my way. It felt so normal, going through security, having a pint outside a WHSmith's while the flight was delayed. I slept through most of the journey, and woke up to the glittering, impossible beauty of Antigua.

The heat when I emerged at the other end was like a blanket. Michael was there to meet me, and we chatted idly all the way back to his house. It was blissfully calm. Michael's house was on the edge of English Harbour. It was so beautiful I felt almost close to tears. There were still good things in the world, I thought. Not everything was gone.

That first weekend, I mostly did the same things I'd been doing at home; sleeping, reading, sitting quietly. The difference was that I was actually calm. Being in Antigua removed me from the real world. It could have been basically any time in my adult life; I could be on holiday from doing anything. I didn't have to wake up every morning and look at my wardrobe full of three-piece suits that I didn't need to wear any more. I just got up and hacked a pineapple into cubes with a pleasingly enormous knife, and sat on the veranda, working my way slowly but surely through

Michael's comprehensive collection of Agatha Christie novels. In the afternoons I went for long walks along the harbour, and looked at the boats, and allowed my brain to think of nothing, to drift peacefully, to do nothing more strenuous than appreciate how pleasing it was to see bright white sails against a bright blue sky.

And then Claire arrived.

I was walking back up the drive to the house when I noticed that Michael's car was parked in a slightly different place. My sun-drunk mind failed to connect the dots, so when I walked into the kitchen I wasn't thinking about anything apart from whether there were any slices of lime left to plunk into the neck of a beer.

"There you are, James," Michael said. "I was wondering where you'd got to. You know Claire, don't you?"

Claire was standing against the kitchen island, a glass of wine in hand. She was wearing an oversized shirt and chinos and one of those huge floppy hats that you only ever see on holiday. She looked much less drawn than the last time I'd seen her; she was visibly tired, but in the way that people are after a long flight, rather than the exhaustion of stress and grief. She was heartbreakingly beautiful.

"I do," I said. I couldn't work out what to do – did I shake her hand? Kiss her cheek?

Claire solved the problem for me by putting down her glass of wine and giving me a hug. For a fleeting second, all I could think about was the lavender smell of her, clean and familiar, and then we broke apart and I tried to kick my brain back into some semblance of normality.

"I suggested she go and lie down, but she claims to have slept on the plane," Michael said, seemingly oblivious. "So, I was thinking we could go and have dinner at Sorrel's, what do you think?"

"Sounds excellent," I said, "let me go and change into something slightly less shabby."

"Oh, me too," Claire said.

"Claire, I stuck your suitcase in the room across from James'," Michael said. He had turned to open the fridge. "D'you mind showing her where it is, James?"

"Of course," I said.

And so we were alone. We walked in silence out of the kitchen and up the stairs. Our rooms were on one side of the house, looking out over the cliff to the sea; Michael's room was on the other, with the hallway and an open veranda and two bathrooms between them. I paused outside the door to my room, and turned back to look at Claire. She was already looking at me. I had no idea what to say.

"James," she said. Her voice was quiet, but there was no chance of my missing a single word. "I know it's not helpful, but…I'm really pleased to see you."

"I'm pleased to see you, too," I said, equally quietly.

"I know – I know we need to talk about some things," she said. "But can we…can we just pretend that everything is OK, just for a little bit? I just…" Her voice shook slightly. "I would just really, really like for everything to be OK for a little bit."

I couldn't help myself. I stepped forward, and kissed her forehead so gently she could barely have felt it.

"We can absolutely do that," I said. "Let's go and eat our body weight in swordfish steaks, hey?"

Claire smiled. "Sounds perfect."

And for three days, it was.

We swam. We lay in the sun. We went on boat trips. We walked on the beach. We walked up to the top of Shirley's Heights. For three whole days, it was as if the rest of the world had fallen away.

Just after breakfast on the fourth day, Claire said that she wanted to walk along the beach and go for a swim in the bay. We waved her goodbye, and I sat on the veranda for a few hours, reading and sipping an aqua fresca.

When two hours had passed since Claire had left, I began to wonder where she was. After three, I wandered down the hill to the beach. She was not on a deckchair, not on the beach, not swimming among the moored boats. She had vanished.

I ran back up to the house. Michael was out of the shower having returned from his late morning walk, and so we ran back to the mooring, where Michael swam out to his RIB, untied it and picked me up from the jetty. We motored around the bay, trying to see if she was in the water. Nothing.

In the next hour, we knocked on the side of every boat in the bay, asking if they had seen anything unusual. Other than a powerful speedboat that was motoring slowly around the bay, no one saw anything.

It came to this: either she had got into difficulty, despite being a strong swimmer, and had somehow drowned without making any sort of sound, which was vanishingly unlikely, or she had been taken.

No, I thought. *No, not again. Surely not. Please, God. Not Claire.*

There was nothing else to do. I called Todd.

"What's up mate?" he asked.

"Claire has been kidnapped. I need help. Whoever you've got out here, please get them mobilised."

"Why do you say that she has been kidnapped?" Todd asked, immediately all business. "Tell me her exact movements until her disappearance."

I set out what we had done since dinner last night. He had in the meantime pulled up an image of the bay in front of Michael's house so he could see what I was talking about. I explained the routine, and how it was normal to go for a morning swim in the bay. She had done that and vanished.

"Right," he said. "I'll need to make some phone calls. If you've called the police, try and get them to come in plain clothes. I'll call you back in fifteen minutes."

And so I waited. I paced the floor. I felt sick. And then I waited some more.

Eventually an elderly Toyota wheezed up the drive. Two men got out, one in his fifties, the other much younger. Both were dressed for the beach. We waved them up onto the veranda.

"Good morning," said the older man. "I'm Chief Superintendent Thompson, and this is Sergeant Byam. I understand that you have reason to believe that one of your guests has been kidnapped."

I let Michael do the talking. He explained Claire's movements and what we had done so far to find her. The two of them were debating the seriousness of the situation when Todd called me back.

"OK. Our local guy is on it, and a colleague is on the next flight from Miami to Antigua. He'll arrive late tonight, go and pick him up – his name's Doug. Have you spoken to the local police?"

"They're here now."

"Let me talk to them." I handed my mobile phone to the Chief Superintendent. He listened to what Todd had to say, occasionally asking a question. Eventually he handed the phone back to me.

"James, mate, you have to assume you're being watched," Todd said. "Try to act normally. Do the sort of things that you've been doing. We'll post a man near the house, so you should be OK. Chin up, mate. Listen to what Tommo says. He seems pretty sensible." With that, he rang off.

The day crawled past. I lay on a deckchair for ten minutes, then got up. Then lay down again. I picked up the book I was reading, but although my eyes went down the page, nothing went in. Even Michael, not normally stationary for more than a few seconds, lay on a deckchair for a bit. Conversation was slow. Lunch came and went. Neither of us had an appetite. Eventually we picked at a picnic supper exhumed from the fridge, and sat in near silence on the veranda, allowing the mosquitoes a clear run at our lower legs.

Finally, it was time to go to the airport. It was almost deserted. We sat quietly, both unable to speak, unable do anything but wait. After an hour, my co-rescuer from Morocco came through the gates and headed straight over to us.

"Doug?" said Michael.

He nodded. The three of us walked silently to the car. Without traffic, we were back at Michael's in forty minutes.

Initially Doug busied himself on his mobile phone. He asked me a few questions about Claire's movements and what her mobile phone number was. Unfortunately, her mobile was still sitting on the table by the side of her bed, so no chance of a beacon to follow this time. Having obtained Michael's permission to borrow the car to meet the flight in the morning, he told us to go to bed.

It was impossible to sleep. I kept thinking what I might have done differently. Who had I not spotted keeping an eye on us? Although the resort at the bottom of Michael's drive was, in theory, bankrupt and therefore semi-dilapidated, in fact there were many holiday homes built round the edge of it, more every year. There were always people milling about; pool attendants, anti-pest sprayers, beach sweepers, water taxi men, cleaners, or actual holidaymakers. As for keeping an eye on us – well, Michael's place was surrounded by bush. You could monitor our comings and goings without leaving a trace.

I lay there and sweated. Eventually I heard Michael's car start; Doug was leaving for the airport. Despite the imminent arrival of the cavalry, and the fact that Antigua is a fraction of the size of Morocco, all I could feel was despair. Being kidnapped had been easier than this. I thought of Claire's reaction when I first saw her after getting back from Morocco, and I finally understood it.

I gave up on sleeping, and went to sit on the veranda. After a while, Michael appeared. As mates we usually talked all the time and laughed like children. We sat in silence until Michael's car pulled up the drive.

To my complete surprise, Todd climbed out of the car. I was fiercely glad to see him; had he been less of a bloke, I would have hugged him. He came straight over to me, and clapped me on the shoulder. There was a wordless moment of complete sympathy, and then he and Doug were gone, disappearing into the bush around the house without a word.

Left to ourselves, Michael and I discussed what to do. Staring in silence at each other was not much of an option; repeating yesterday's sit down, get up, sit down on the deckchairs didn't appeal either.

"Stuff this," said Michael, "if we've been spied on, let's try and work out from where."

English Harbour is a natural bay. Approaching from the sea, the Pillars of Hercules are on the right, at the bottom of the cliffs that edge Shirley's Heights. On the left is a finger of land which had, at one time, had a gun emplacement on it; there was still an ammunition store standing. Dead ahead is the beach, with Michael's house set back and slightly to the left. The bay bears round to the left, and houses Nelson's Dockyard, which comprises the now restored 18th century buildings originally used as maintenance shops for the fleet.

Behind Michael's house the land rises sharply. Although there are properties above and behind it, the scrub was so dense that it would make a poor observation platform. But if you set off from the house heading east and walked through the derelict resort towards the Yacht Club flagpole, there was plenty of virgin scrub there in which to hide.

We stood by the pool, working out fields of vision.

"That's where I'd be," Michael said, pointing towards the flagpole.

And so we went. Despite the heat we pulled on long trousers; the scrub is part cactus, part thorn and all sharp spikes, so shorts were a no-no. Michael dived into his garage and emerged with a machete and his bird watching binoculars.

In the target zone there were a number of paths; stray off them, and the scrub was pretty dense. We figured that what we were looking for would be difficult to see but easy to access. We hacked our way through the scrub, periodically looking back at the house via the binoculars to establish how much of the property we could see. It dawned on us that with the way it was laid out behind other properties and the surrounding trees, the site of the vantage point would be in a relatively small area. It was tough work, but at least we were doing something.

We paused to share a bottle of water, and I looked back down at the bay. "We're attacking this from below," I said. "But the path runs from the flagpole all the way up to the top of Shirley's Heights. Why don't we start from up there, and come at it from above? That way there may be easier access to the spot."

Michael nodded. "Good idea."

We circled round on the existing path, going uphill, above where we judged the vantage point to be. Within minutes we found it. It was a small clearing, just big enough to house a man in a chair. We squatted down. The view of the house, through the binoculars, was near perfect. Judging from the marks on the floor the spy had been there for a while. Better, lying on the floor, partly covered by soil, was an empty crisp packet.

One more piece of the puzzle.

Doug and Todd had burst out laughing when we told them with some pride that we had procured another car from a mate of Michael's. An ancient Daewoo finished in rust with small patches of white, inside the sun-damaged upholstery had disintegrated completely. The remedy had been to fill the seat frame with old newspapers tied up with string and put a cushion on the top. "That pile of shit? I wondered why that was there. You can't seriously expect any of us to use that?"

Doug silently motioned for the keys and went down to the driveway. He looked under the bonnet, poked and prodded some of the all-too-fragile bodywork, got in and started it up. He reversed out into the road, disappearing for twenty minutes. When he got back and joined us, all he said was, "It's OK."

"Right," said Todd. "You get your car back. We'll use the Aston. No one will nick it and it is good cover. It looks pretty shit, though. Will the police stop us for want of the local MOT?" he asked.

"It's got one," said Michael. "Sticker in the bottom of the windscreen. I know it's no thing of beauty, but it works OK. And it'll be safe."

We didn't see much of Todd and Doug, although I texted Doug the location of the lookout spot. Todd replied by asking if Michael had any contacts with the harbour authorities. The answer was yes; and so Michael disappeared, and I was left alone with my gnawing fear.

Late in what seemed to be an endless afternoon, my phone rang. "Can I speak to James Westerfeld, please?" said a posh voice.

"Speaking," I replied.

"It's Torquil Evans-Jones here, secretary to the Duke of Richmond. I thought that you would like to know that we have found Mr Akely's holdall."

This couldn't seem less important, but my manners took over. "Oh, excellent," I said. "Where was it?"

"After the Revival Meeting it can take a day or so before people take their stuff out of the changing room. The bag was the last thing left. The cleaners were aware that it might belong to the driver who had died, and had put it in the store cupboard of the airfield clubhouse to keep it safe. And then they forgot to mention it to anyone. One of them was cleaning the Duke's study and overheard a conversation His Grace was having with someone on the phone – she remembered about the bag and told him. Poor thing – she thought she was in trouble for not having mentioned it before."

"On the contrary," I said, "give her a raise."

"We thought you would be pleased. What would you like us to do with it?"

I managed to dredge up a sensible answer. "Send it to PC O'Dwyer of Sussex Police. Do you have his details?" I asked

"Somewhere, yes." Torquil hummed, and I could almost see him making a note. "How is Mrs Akely coping?"

I closed my eyes. "She's fine," I said. "Recovering. I know that she'll be pleased to hear about his things, and I'm very grateful to you all for your help."

"Don't mention it, old man." He hung up.

Sleep came slowly that night, and not for too long. The next thing I was aware of was Doug shaking me awake.

"James. Get up. We need you."

I was in my T-shirt and shorts in seconds and found him, Michael and Todd on the veranda. Todd and Doug were dressed entirely in black, with rolled-up balaclavas on the backs of their heads.

"Take a seat," said Todd. "We think we know where Claire is – it's a yacht out in the harbour. It's been moored there for a while, but we heard the crew discussing orders to sail. We aren't sure when they will do that – probably at first light. So we need to move now.

"Doug and I will get on board, but we need the two of you to help. We want you, Michael, to cause a diversion by trying to get on board up the rear gangplank. There'll be a member of the crew on watch and we want you to keep that person occupied. Do you have a blazer and trousers you can wear?"

"Yes, I do," he said.

"Good. Go and put them on. We want you to pretend to be someone official." Michael went to his room.

"James, we want you back on land in the Aston as back-up, and to cause a diversion if necessary after we have got clear of the boat. Clear?"

"Yes," I said. "How are you going to get on board?"

"Let us worry about that. While Michael's occupying the crew at the back of the boat, we'll be busy at the front."

"Is it parked stern on like the others?" I asked.

"*Moored* stern *to*? Yes it is."

"What time is it?" I asked.

"3.10am. We go as soon as Michael is dressed."

He reappeared in seconds, looking very official, and we headed off, Doug and Michael in his Toyota and Todd and me in the Aston. On the short run to the harbour, Todd was silent. He told me to park in the main car park, wait until he got back, and if there were pursuers to try to lead them further into the island. Michael had parked next to the petrol station on the main road, no doubt on Doug's instruction. I got out of the car with Todd and walked with him the few yards to the water's edge. There, tied to a hoop in the sea wall, was a small inflatable boat.

Doug appeared, and the two of them rolled down their balaclavas. They slipped into the boat and paddled silently to the front of a large yacht parked in the middle of a line of destroyer-sized monsters. Seconds later I could make out the shape of two dark figures climbing up the front anchor chain.

I stood and waited. The only noise to start with was the chirruping of the cicadas. Then I heard Michael, suddenly possessed of a smart English accent, calling out.

"Is there anybody there? I'm coming aboard."

To start with there was no reaction; but then the lights at the stern of the boat came on, and two figures in dark blue polo shirts and white Bermuda shorts. I couldn't hear every word but it was clear that what he was saying was causing no small consternation.

"Even if you are right, why are we discussing this at three o'clock in the morning?" one of the crew said. Michael's response was a bit muffled but I heard the word "permit". Another light went on, and a third crew member joined them. From his accent he was Italian, and his arrival ramped up the volume of the discussion. He was not happy.

Then lights went on in the two boats either side, and I could hear shouted questions from other crew members.

The Italian voice started to make "get off our boat" noises, but Michael was having none of it. Another voice, female and English, was suddenly audible.

"Come back at 10am, and we can sort this out then."

I was starting to worry that Michael would be forced off the boat before the end of the need for the diversion. At that moment I saw a figure climbing down the anchor chain, carrying a largeish pack on his back, with a second figure following shortly afterwards.

The "discussion" at the back of the yacht now involved the word "police". No one seemed to act on that suggestion, but more importantly there was no unexpected noise or lights from the front of the vessel. The small dinghy rowed quietly up to where I was standing. One of them tied it onto the hoop and jumped effortlessly up onto the jetty. He turned and held out his arms for the bag, which he slung over his shoulder.

"Is it Claire?" I asked.

"Yes of course it fucking is." Todd said. "Get moving!"

I had the car moving as fast as I could, the revs causing a racket. "Straight home?" I asked.

He pulled up the balaclava and grinned at me in the mirror. "Straight home."

Nothing followed behind us, although Michael couldn't have been far off.

"Does she need a doctor?" I asked.

"We gave her a whiff of something to knock her out to avoid an ill-timed scream. I think she's OK. Our organisation has a doctor on the island. As soon as we get back we'll contact her and get her to come."

Our speed on the journey was only moderated by the appalling state of the Antiguan roads. Before I had the car stopped Todd was hauling Claire out of the car. She groaned softly. With surprising grace, he laid her down on the table and grabbed a cushion to put under her head. She groaned again and mumbled something I couldn't catch.

Sleep was going to be impossible, so I put the kettle on and suggested coffee. From there, things were a bit of a blur. The doctor arrived first and made Todd carry Claire to bed before kicking us all out of the room. It seemed an age before she emerged, but the news was a relief; apart from some bruising around her neck and red marks all over from being restrained, she seemed all right. The doctor left me her number and made it clear that anything other than a rapid recovery should involve me calling her without delay.

I headed back to the veranda where Todd, Doug and Michael were drinking more coffee.

"Tell me," I said.

Todd nodded.

With Michael making a proper and audible nuisance of himself at the stern of the boat, he and Doug had climbed up onto the prow. From there they moved silently down the far side, heading towards the back, until they reached the balcony for the next deck down. From there they headed forward and down, reasoning that the most likely place for a prisoner would be the forward sailing locker.

Like all modern super yachts, it never really slept, so they were accompanied by the constant hum of pumps and air conditioning compressors, which helped mask the noise of their footsteps.

Lying on some boxes, hands tied, was Claire, semi-conscious. Doug knocked her out completely, hefted her over his shoulder, and the two of them retraced their steps. They'd been back with me within minutes.

"Thank you," I said. Todd and Doug looked at me, and both nodded. And that was all we ever said about it.

By now it was 6am and getting light. I couldn't bear not being able to see Claire any longer. I slipped away from the others, who were discussing the merits of a fry-up to calm the nerves, and headed up to her room.

She was lying in bed when I walked in, but she was awake. Her head was partially bandaged, and there were still some flecks of blood in her white-blonde hair. She was sitting up slightly, looking out of the window at the sunrise.

"James," she said, without looking over at me.

"Claire."

I walked very gently over to the bed, and sat down next to her.

"I knew you'd come for me," she said. She was still looking out over the bay. "Even during the worst of it, I wasn't afraid. Or – no, I was afraid, I was terrified, but I was also completely sure that if I could keep it together, you would come and find me." She paused. "Absolutely certain."

"Claire," I said again. And then she finally turned. Tears were streaming silently down her face, but she was beaming.

"I knew it," she said. "And I was right."

And all at once she had fallen into my arms; and then I wasn't thinking about anything at all.

Afterwards, I lay there for a bit, just watching her. I should have been exhausted, but I felt more alive than I had in weeks. I could see why, if you had the requisite skills, Todd's life was so interesting.

Back on the veranda, laughter had vented the pressure, and suddenly it was a party. Hiding in the back of the fridge were two bottles of fizz; we cracked them both open. Twenty minutes later, Claire emerged, blinking in the early morning sunshine.

I introduced her to Todd and Doug. Todd shook her hand, but Doug got up and kissed it, much like a French nobleman. Even with us all so shaken, exhausted and triumphant, we had the best breakfast party since I was a student.

Around mid-morning, Chief Superintendent Thompson drove up to the house. As we all convened round the big table on the Veranda, including Todd and Doug, we were treated to an informal, off the record update as to what the police had found on the yacht. The crew numbered fifteen. Most were young Brits or Antipodeans spending a few months enjoying being close to the lives of the very rich. The captain was in police custody and not saying much. The first thing the police had done was fingerprint the lot. One of the male deckhands, Italian, possessed fingerprints which matched those found on the crisp packet. He, too was zipped up like a suitcase.

All cabins used by the crew had been searched. In one they found a zip up case which contained syringes and vials of diamorphine. Blood was found on the needles. While it was too early to be sure, no one was betting against the blood being Claire's. The resident of the cabin, evidently known to all as Ripper, had been fingerprinted. His dabs were all over the medical case. He, it seemed, realising that his room for manoeuvre was limited, was busy dobbing the others in. It was he who manned the speed boat. Ripper had whacked Claire on the back of the head with an oar, pulled her onto the floor of the speedboat and drugged her there and then. He then motored gently back to Falmouth Harbour and with some help from two other crew members he had taken her down to the forward locker. He further admitted drugging her on three occasions after she was imprisoned. He did not know, or was not saying, what her ultimate fate was to be. He had named the two assistants who had moved Claire's unconscious body, and they were being held as accessories. Most of the other crew were either oblivious to all this, or at least there was no evidence that they weren't, so they would be released. Tommo was in the process of getting search warrants for a number of the largest vessels moored on the island. He finished by thanking us, and Todd and Doug in particular, for our efforts. Of course, he said, the police could not condone private citizens taking matters into their own hands, but he was realistic enough to see that without us, Claire would still be facing an uncertain future. He also had a decent haul to put before the courts: the captain, the Italian deckhand, Ripper and his two cohorts. Well done all. He then said that, as of now, he was off duty, at which point Michael appeared from the downstairs fridge with another bottle of champagne.

We spent the rest of the holiday quietly: walking, sleeping and swimming. On our last night, I booked a table at Catherine's, arguably the best restaurant in Antigua and bought the five of us a very expensive dinner. Walking back with Claire's hand in mine, the night sky lit up with stars. I thought at that moment, despite everything, I might be entirely happy.

20

The winter ground on, cold, wet and frequently icy. A blanket of cold air had arrived from Russia in mid-February and settled over the south of England.

Todd installed panic buttons at both our homes, but they remained unused. No dark coloured Fords menaced me as I moved about London. Much of my time was spent worrying intensely about the upcoming court case; every time it was delayed I wanted to give up. And yet, when Terry called me in late February asking if I wanted to get the Cortina tuned up before the season started, I said yes. Objectively, this was an insane decision. I was about to go into a trial which would define the rest of my life. I wasn't broke, but I wasn't making any money either; my savings weren't going to last indefinitely. But what kept going through my mind was this: it was entirely possible that I was never going to have the opportunity to race again. It was entirely possible that I was going to be sent to prison for a long, long time for something I didn't do, and that when I finally emerged, I would be too old and broke and worn-down to drive anywhere more exciting than the nearest Sainsbury's. So for as long as I was allowed, I wanted to be who I had been: a man who loved to race.

Terry was in an excellent mood when I arrived. He had a roll-up in one hand and a book of chess problems in the other, his feet up on the table, puffing away contentedly. He showed me a picture of his wife Tracy – resplendent in her best M&S floral shift dress and a haircut that strongly resembled a confused porcupine – holding an enormous trophy.

"All-England Women's," Terry said, proudly. "Beat some squit of a fourteen-year-old prodigy in the final."

He made us both cups of tea, and we headed over to the Cortina. We agreed that as it had been competitive enough, subject to wear and tear, we would leave the engine alone. It didn't smoke or use oil, so I got away with no more than a check-over and an oil change. Historic motor racing was an increasingly competitive business though. Big money had come into the sport which meant that a fast car one season would be midfield the next and not long after that, propping up the grid. So, if power was not going to be increased, what do you do? Changing the differential back to its pre-Spa spec was a given.

"Got an idea to make your car faster," said Terry, when we'd talked that through.

"Oh yes. How so?" I replied.

"Negative camber at the back."

I reached for another teabag. "How does that work? It's a live axle."

"Says here that you can get special hub bearings which splay the wheels out at the bottom. Worth two seconds a lap round the GP circuit at Silverstone."

"That's well worth having," I replied, with my interest well piqued. "What's the catch?"

"The cost," he replied. "You need what is known as a fully floating axle, which involves machining special splines and putting shims in the hubs."

"Good," I said. "I understood quite a lot of that. How expensive is it?"

"With shipping from the US, duty, so on – six and a half grand. Before fitting." He looked at me, eyebrows raised. "Or, you can just bend the axle."

"Are you telling me that an American company has special race parts for a British car that went out of production in 1966?"

"No. I'm telling you that an American company will make you special race parts for your car." He relit his roll-up.

"How would it affect reliability?"

"Well, this set-up is used in NASCAR racing. It's reliable and makes them faster. But it is expensive," he said. "And you don't seem to be rolling in it these days."

I ignored him. "Tell me about bending the axle."

"Much cheaper, nearly the same effect and no massive parts bill," he said. "The idea is that you don't want too much negative camber, maybe one or two degrees. So, what you do is heat the top of the axle casing about five or six inches inboard of the brakes, and let it cool. This contracts the metal. Your axle's now shaped like a banana. The half shafts are running in a casing that's not straight, but that's not a problem because there's enough tolerance where the splines meet the hub bearings for them not to notice. The clever bit is heating the axle just enough and also heating it the same on both sides. You also need about one degree of toe-in, but that I can adjust."

I paused and pondered possibly the longest speech I had ever heard him make. "Can you do that?" I asked.

"I reckon I can," he replied. "I'd have to strip the axle out of the car and take the innards out. But I can do that."

"What happens if you over-do the heat?" I asked.

"You would need a new axle casing. Difficult but not impossible to get. I hope that it wouldn't come to that, but it's a bit like surgery. No guarantees."

"And you think that bending the axle would have the same effect as filling it with fancy American parts?"

"Sure. We've been doing it on the stock cars for the last twenty-five years," he said.

"Done," I said, and he grinned. "Have you got any other clever ideas you've been sitting on?"

"Nah," he laughed. "That's your lot for this year. I have to finish a car that's going out tonight."

-

As good as his word, Terry had the car ready in time for the Goodwood test day. I was looking forward to trying out the mods and seeing what, if any, difference they made. I had also done a bit of homework. At the Easter Monday meeting in 1966, just before the circuit closed, the great Jim Clark was timed at 1.33.2 in his Lotus Cortina. The current BTCC hotshots had taken about three seconds off that, due, in the main, to engineering advances with the cars. The circuit was resurfaced some years ago which flattened some of the bumps, but also, supposedly, made it more slippery. Being neither a BTCC ace nor Jim Clark, I thought a 1.34 would be respectable. In practice for the fatal race last September I had done a 1.35, but there had been a lot of oil on the track. Wilf Steer had done a best of 1.33.5 when he was in my car. So that was the benchmark and target.

I had the car on the trailer outside my house on Friday night and had barely slept with childish excitement at going racing again. For the first time in months, I felt like myself.

Track days at Goodwood involve no more than five cars out at a time, with strict rules as to overtaking; each session lasts five laps. Subject to joining the back of the queue in the pit lane you could go out as much as you wanted, so today was partly huge fun and partly a learning exercise. For some reason I never got as nervous before a track day as I did before a race, which made no sense insofar as I was doing the same thing to the same degree. Perhaps subconsciously I wasn't trying quite as hard.

I was far enough up the queue to be in the second session and keen to learn if Terry's mods had affected the way the car handled and steered. Lap 1 was a sighter, not least because while the engine had been warmed through the drive train, the tyres and the brakes were still cold. By the chicane things were coming together and I passed the pits at full chat. Madgwick, the first corner after the pits, is another double apex right hander, but with a bump on the way out. So, dab the brakes, slip into third and flick it in. The car turned in slightly more reluctantly which I took as a sign that there was now more grip at the back. What hadn't changed was the car's wonderful ability to simply flow into oversteer where, almost without noticing, you find yourself sideways but under full control. Christ, this thing would make anyone look good!

I cruised over the bump, changed up at 7,800 rpm and ran down to Fordwater. Being in a properly fast car Fordwater is a challenge. In a Lotus Cortina it's a kink. By the right hander leading into St Marys I was nearing full speed. I could *just* take this flat, but a bit like Eau Rouge at Spa, it would be a mistake to do so, because of what comes next. St Marys is the only left hander, and while reasonably quick you have to be careful on the exit because the road falls away from you and it is easy to spin here. As with everywhere else at Goodwood, the run-off, if you get it wrong, is limited. The fastest way I had found was a dab of the brakes on the way in, get over to the right side of the track and change down to third before turning left. Once again turn-in was slightly delayed but again it flowed into oversteer.

From there you head downhill, back in top to Lavant; this is two corners with a short straight between them. In fact, get it right and it can be drifted through as one long corner. Exit speed is important as that factors your ultimate speed down the Lavant Straight (which is anything but straight) as you approach Woodecote. This was the corner where Bill was killed and I nearly crashed in sympathy. Then there is the chicane and the whole joy starts again. By now I was really on it, and found that as I got used to the handling changes, I could get on the power sooner after braking for a corner.

Timing cars at track days in theory is *verboten*, but I had left a box of tricks on the pit wall which communicated with a data logger in the car, hidden up behind the dashboard so as not spoil the purist 1960s look of the interior. After four and a half laps I slowed down to cool the car before I had to stop it. I had learned the hard way some years before that if you thrashed a car until the last moment and then simply switched it off, with the water no longer circulating round the engine the heat build-up would firstly push the water out of the overflow, and then melt the head gasket because by now there was no coolant in the car. If you really ballsed it up you could bend the cylinder head, rendering it scrap.

Once back in the queue I kept the engine running for three or four minutes so as to let the heat bleed away. Only then did I retrieve my gizmo and have a look at the data. It was a cool, still and, crucially, dry day, so pretty much perfect for what we were doing. No excuses there then. 1.32.9!

I climbed out and was drinking a bottle of water – though the prospect of just dumping it over my head was also pretty appealing – when I saw them. They were both huge blokes, well over six feet, dressed to blend in with the crowd but still fairly conspicuous. And they were watching me.

I slowly screwed the cap back onto my water and assessed my options. Todd was back in the paddock, cheerfully holding forth to Terry about the many merits of Australia. I'd been surprised he'd been so calm about me going racing, but when I'd said as much, he'd just laughed.

"I'm going to check the ever-living shit out of that rust bucket you call a race car," he said. "And then, to be honest, I'm going to relax. The one place no self-respecting villain is going to come for you is in front of thousands of people at fucking Goodwood."

But now I wished he was here. The way they were looking at me sent cold shivers down my spine. I finished up the last few tasks as quickly as possible, and then headed out to find the others. I checked the reflection in a passing car, and saw that the two men were following me as I left. My shoulders tightened, but I tried to seem natural as I walked a little faster, then faster still. By the time I'd reached Terry and Todd, who were both laughing about something, I was almost jogging.

"James, mate," Todd said. "What the fuck's got into you?"

"Two blokes," I said. "I think – those two blokes behind me, they're following me."

Todd and Terry both ducked around me to look.

"There's no-one there," Terry said.

I turned to look. He was right; the two men had vanished. Todd was looking at me carefully.

"There were two blokes!" I said. "Big, scary-looking blokes." Both of them were now looking at me. "I'm serious!"

"I'm sure you are," Todd said. "But they're not here now."

I caught the sliver of something on Terry's face that I realised was pity. I realised all at once how I must sound; how I must look to him.

"You did a good run," Terry said. "That bent axle worked a treat, eh?"

I took one last look behind me and then I made a very conscious effort to turn back to him. There was nothing there. There was nothing to worry about.

"Some of your better work," I said, and Terry laughed, and started asking questions about the oversteer. But I couldn't quite lose track of Todd's thoughtful expression as he scanned the crowd, watching for something that might not be there.

21

Then all the fun was over, and I had to – finally – focus on the trial for real. Sara had agreed to continue representing me, even though every time we spoke it became more and more obvious that she believed I'd completely lost my marbles. She'd instructed a junior of exactly my call, which was oddly galling; the chances of something as juicy as this ever coming across my desk were vanishingly small. The junior's name was David Tsang. He had a beautiful RP accent that sounded exactly like he was about to announce that the BBC's fine televisual entertainment would soon be available in colour, and if he made less than four times my average annual earnings, I was a satsuma. He was at one of the Bedford Row sets that mostly handled bafflingly complex white-collar crime and flashy, gruesome murders. In essence: Sara had found me a thoroughbred. David had listened to the entirety of my story with an expression so exquisitely neutral that I wanted to ask him for tips on how to achieve it; and then, not entirely to my surprise, he implied heavily that my best bet would be to plead guilty now, reap the early plea benefit, become deeply remorseful, and hope for a judge who had a soft spot for junior barristers.

"I didn't do it, though," I said.

"Which means that of course I must advise you to plead not guilty," David said, smooth as a BSB spokesman. "You know the rules perfectly well, James. I'm just making sure you understand the full extent of the prosecution's case."

Which, in his defence, was pretty substantial. It wasn't a complicated case. I'd been identified by an eyewitness with no previous, good eyesight, and a sterling reputation; we didn't even bother to dispute the fact that it was clearly my details that had been used to rent the lockup, because even the dimmest jury wasn't going to buy that there had been two James Westerfeld's born in the same cottage hospital on the same day with the same driving licence. Handwriting experts had decreed that the rental agreement was in my handwriting. It was open and shut.

-

"Isn't there something you can do about this?"

Todd and I were sitting in the garden. He'd asked how the meeting with David and Sara had gone, and I'd just moaned for the length of two beers about the whole thing.

"What kind of thing did you have in mind?" Todd asked.

"I don't know," I said. "You're the one who's dropped into my life like fucking James Bond. Prove I didn't do it with some gadget given to you by Q. Hell, provide some handy truth serum we can shoot into that pillock from the lockup with a dart gun just before he takes the stand."

Todd was grinning. "I can ask Mustapha about our gadgets department," he said. "But to be honest I always thought James Bond was a bit of a prat. Most of what you need to get business done you can find in a climbing shop run by pothead nineteen-year-olds."

"I don't even want to begin to think about what 'business' means in this context," I said.

"Smart man." Todd tipped his beer to me. "But, on a more serious note, mate – there's stuff going on behind the scenes. Stuff you don't know, and stuff I don't know. All I can say for sure is that Mustapha isn't planning to let someone as useful as you rot in prison for thirty years."

"Useful?" Because I'm vain, this was the first thing I heard. "I'm not – hang on, what did any of that mean?"

Todd grinned again. "James, mate. You know I'm not going to tell you."

"This cloak-and-dagger shit looked much more fun in the movies," I said, grumpily, and Todd laughed. "No but, seriously, what the hell use could I be to Mustapha?"

Todd was now playing with a carabiner he kept clipped to the belt loop of his jeans; making it dance across his hand, spinning it, flicking it so it closed in mid-air. It was such a casual display of astonishing dexterity that I almost couldn't focus on what he was saying.

"You're a barrister," Todd said. "So, you know a good bit about the law. Could probably learn the laws of some other places, if you needed to. And you sound like a lawyer. Given IDs aren't exactly an issue, I can think of a thousand uses for you."

"Fuck," I said.

"You said it," Todd said. "Look, you basically never do what I tell you to and it's a fucking pain in the arse. For once in your life listen to me when I say: you do not want to fuck with Mustapha."

"Oh God no," I said. "I am not planning to."

"Good," Todd said. "You're a fucking stupid Pom and you've got the wine palate of a bogan, but it's easier to cadge beers off you while you've still got fingers."

-

Later that week I was sitting up in my study, staring up through the skylight at an uncharacteristically blue March sky, not thinking about much of anything. Given that my state of mind was otherwise a kind of queasy panic, this was actually quite pleasant. It was broken by my phone ringing.

"Hello?"

"James?" I recognised the voice, but couldn't place it.

"Speaking."

"It's Clive Mitcham – from the customs office."

"Clive!" I sat back in my chair. "How are you?"

"Well, thanks," Clive said. "I'd ask how you're doing, but I get the impression the answer is 'piss-poor'."

"Not basically wrong," I said. "What can I do for you?"

Clive paused, and then sighed, a short, frustrated huff of breath. "Right. Look, I really shouldn't be telling you any of this."

"I know."

"And you can't go blabbing about it."

"I know."

"OK." He paused again. "I had dinner with my brother last night. We'd had a few drinks, and then a couple more, and your name came up."

"How on earth did my name come up?"

Clive sighed again, this time a little more gently. "The thing about Harry is that he can't let anything go," he said. "Ever since he was a kid. If there's something he doesn't understand he just worries away at it like a dog with a stick. He wanted to be a detective – that's how he ended up doing this. And don't get me wrong, he's a damn fine officer as a result. If he thinks something's dodgy he won't stop until he's figured it out."

"Right," I said. "So?"

"So, this whole business with those Akely's got under his skin," Clive said. "He kept digging. It bothered him that he didn't know who'd tipped them off, so he talked to friends, and looked through the records, and did something I don't understand with computers, and after a lot of futzing about on his own time he found the phone number that had called in the tip."

I almost dropped the phone. "You're kidding."

"I am not," Clive said. "He called it, obviously, but didn't get anything – turns out it's a phone box. Blast from the past, eh? Do you have a pen? I'll give you the address."

I could feel my insides knotting with excitement, and I scrambled for a pen. "Go for it."

"It's in West Norfolk," he said. "Just outside the post office in some hamlet called West Dereham."

"I – " Surprise hit like a sledgehammer. "Are you sure?"

"Positive," Clive said. "Harry mentioned it twice because West Dereham is where Akely was from. He figures some local dipshit put their girlfriend up to it as a lark that got out of hand."

My stomach dropped. "Put – hang on, put his girlfriend up to it?"

"Yeah," Clive said. "That was the other thing. It was a female voice on the phone."

22

It was a long drive to Norfolk. The traffic was bad around Newmarket, slowed in places to a complete standstill by some construction work. Todd was driving. This was partly because he rarely let me drive the Senator anywhere anymore, pointing out, quite correctly, that it had all bulletproof qualities of wet tissue paper; but it was mostly because my hands were shaking so violently that I couldn't have driven even if he'd let me. He hadn't asked why we were suddenly going to Norfolk. After asking where to go, he hadn't said anything at all. He was a man who knew how to be quiet in high-stress situations, and so he was. He shut up, and drove.

We reached the Akely's a little after seven. As we parked, I could see Claire giving Eleanor and Jake their tea; her hair was loose down her back, and the children were laughing. The sun had set, and now it was dark everywhere but that kitchen. Claire looked up when she heard the car wheels crunching on the gravel. She said something to the children, and then crossed to open the door to the yard.

"Hello?" She squinted in the darkness, and then the yard lights flicked on, and she visibly relaxed. "Jesus, James, you nearly gave me a heart attack. Why didn't you say you were – " But she'd stopped talking because she'd seen my face.

"Todd," I said. "Could you go and entertain the kids for a bit?"

"On it," Todd said. Claire let him past. He'd met the kids before, when he'd come up to install the panic button; with the uncritical taste of small children everywhere, they had adored him. This was probably because he told them wildly unsuitable stories about adventures hunting snakes and crocodiles and giant child-eating spiders in the Australian outback.

"Come into the office," Claire said. Her voice was very quiet. "Everyone's gone home for the minute."

So we walked in silence through the yard, over to the office. It was just as tidy as it had been when I first visited, every spanner, bolt and file in its correct place. Claire closed the door behind me, and then we were alone.

"Claire," I said. "I have to ask you something, and I need you to tell me the truth."

Claire opened her mouth to speak, but nothing came out. She nodded.

"I have reason to believe you were the one who tipped customs off about the drugs in Bill's trucks," I said. "It's good reason too. So I'm only going to ask you this once. Did you?"

Claire closed her eyes for a long second, and I looked at the way her lashes curved against her cheek, and I could feel my heart breaking.

"Yes," she said, very quietly. "Yes, it was me who called them. I rang them from a phone box in the village the day before Bill was due to come back."

In all my years of practice, I'd met a lot of violent people. I'd never understood what motivated them; what forces must have been raging inside them to make them behave that way. At that moment, I understood. I wanted nothing more than to sweep every perfect box off the perfect shelves and scatter the contents to the winds.

"Why?" I asked. I was proud of how neutral my voice was. It was a barrister's voice.

Claire bit her lip and I could tell she was trying not to cry. It was a testament to my anger that this didn't do anything to me.

"I found drugs in one of the trucks," she said. Her voice was still very quiet and shaking, but she was holding it together. "I was looking for an earring I'd lost earlier in the day and crawled under a table and there they were, half hidden behind a loose bit of panelling. I just sat there and pulled them out, looked at them. It's the stupidest thing, but I'd never actually seen drugs before, apart from some weed one of my cousins offered me when I was a kid. I couldn't – I mean, there was nothing else they could be. There's no other reason you'd hide something like that." She paused, swallowed. "Bill found me. Came looking for me because Jake needed his swimming kit for the morning and Bill didn't know where I kept his goggles. He found me sitting on the floor of the truck, kilos of heroin in my lap, just looking at them."

I didn't say anything.

"I've never been so furious in my whole life," she said. "I was livid. To think he'd brought this to our house – to somewhere our kids played, somewhere any client could see – I couldn't believe he was that stupid. And more than that, I was shocked. Bill was – Bill was a bloody Boy Scout. His favourite drink was a shandy. He disapproved of the boys in the shop swearing. The man ironed his pants. He was the world's least likely drug dealer."

She took a deep breath. "So, I asked him, and he came and sat down next to me on the floor, and he didn't say anything for a long while. And then he explained. He'd overspent on the trucks – way overspent, in fact, far more than I'd realised. We weren't going to make it unless something changed. And then – then something did. Someone offered him a lot of money – a *lot* of money – if he'd help them get their stuff through customs. No-one searches trucks like these properly; drivers come through customs almost every week. The officers don't even look inside most of the time."

"So you decided to dob in your husband?" I asked.

Claire turned to look at me and there was fury in her expression as well as devastation.

"You have no idea what I went through," she said. "He was getting phone calls all hours of the night. People were threatening him. I knew – I knew he was fighting them. Trying to stop. But they didn't want to. He'd wake up in the middle of the night, shaking, convinced that someone was coming for him. And he wasn't a paranoid man, my husband. He made his whole living on calculating risk accurately. If he thought he was in danger, he was. And I knew it would be so easy to cause an accident. He was a driver; drivers get hurt all the time."

She lifted up her head. Her eyes were shining with tears, but her jaw was firm.

"So I did what I thought was best," I said. "I gave an anonymous tip to the customs people, knowing Bill wouldn't expect it. I thought they'd catch him, and put him safely in custody, and then he'd be able to tell them who was running this and they'd catch them and we would be safe. I thought that if he could give them a whole drug smuggling operation, they'd let him go. That I could have my husband back." Tears had begun to run down her face, but her voice was steady. "We'd worked so hard, James. We'd built a life together from almost nothing. I wasn't just going to let it disappear."

"But it didn't work," I said. "Customs didn't find anything."

"They didn't," Claire said. "Dumb luck, as it turns out. It just happened to be a clean run. Bill was so relieved. But I was – I was scared, then. Because whoever it was that was watching him must know that someone knew. They knew he was a liability now."

She looked up at the ceiling, trying to blink back the tears. "I begged him not to race at Goodwood, James. I knew – God, I just knew something would happen. When his car hit the bank, it was almost a relief; the worst had happened."

"I'm sorry," I said. "Truly I am. But – Claire, why did you get me involved in this? You pretended – you must have *known* I would be in danger if I got involved. You knew this was going to go badly. Why – what on earth possessed you to bring me into this?"

Claire closed her eyes. "It was because you're a barrister," she said. "When they told me a barrister had seen the crash – it was too good an opportunity to miss. I thought that – I thought that you would know people, know things about crime that I don't, know what to do about all this. So I asked you to help, and because you are a good man, you did. You helped, and kept helping."

I felt the cold, physically felt it, in the pit of my stomach. "So none of this was real," I said. "You chose me because you thought I'd be useful. You invited me here, and you were so confused, you needed my help – and all this time, you knew. You knew exactly where those payments came from. You knew, you *knew*, that by involving me in this – were you even surprised when I got kidnapped?" She didn't say anything. "And all that because – because you thought I was *useful*? You played me like a fool."

And now she looked up, and her expression was savage. "And weren't you *easy* to play?" she spat. "Coming up here, the big man, looking after the poor little widow. Oh, poor Claire, so *vulnerable*, so *fragile*, a little girl lost in a big scary world of men and cars. So easy to get you to want to look after me, because you were so obviously getting off on being the hero."

"I'm sorry that my good intentions were so predictable," I said. "And I must commend you on your acting."

"I wasn't acting, you fucking *pillock*," she said. "I'd just lost my husband. I thought we were going to spend the rest of our lives together – I thought we were going to grow old and argue about where to go on cruises, I thought we'd wait together to see our grandkids for the first time. I *was* devastated. And I *don't* know anything about sodding cars, and I *was* overwhelmed, and exhausted, and grateful for the help."

"But I was just a convenience," I said. "Someone who – and everything between us. It was all a play, then. To keep me in, to distract focus from you. What happened in Antigua…none of it was real."

"That's the worst part," Claire said. All at once, the fight had gone out of her; she was suddenly about a foot shorter, thin, exhausted, pale as fog. Her voice was quiet. "It was real, James. How I felt about you – after Portugal, after you disappeared – it was real. When you came up here afterwards, when you got back – the relief, I thought I would collapse. God, James, it was real."

"Well, in the unlikely event that that's true, I'm very sorry to hear it," I said. My tone was utterly neutral. "It's clearly been a very difficult few months for you, and I apologise if I've added to that in any way."

Claire looked like I'd slapped her. "James…"

"I'll be leaving now," I said. "I'd appreciate it if you didn't try to contact me. I'll be very busy, these next few weeks, trying to make sure I don't go to prison. If by some miracle I manage to salvage what's left of my life, I'm sure you'll read about it in the papers."

"James, please – "

"Goodbye, Claire."

I turned and walked away. I didn't look back. I couldn't bear to go into the house, so I stood next to the car and yelled for Todd, and he came outside swiftly.

"You done, mate?" he asked.

I nodded. "Oh yes," I said. "I'm done."

23

The only other case I had on the stocks was defending a murder at the Old Bailey. The facts were all too depressingly familiar. South London is divided up by, to white eyes, invisible boundaries between gangs. However, to the predominantly black residents the dividing lines were all too real. Each gang's turf was jealously guarded, and it was a brave or foolhardy individual from the "wrong" crew who ventured into a neighbouring patch. That had happened in September the previous year and one Junior Managwa had left his home area, governed by the Kennington Homies, and travelled to Stockwell, run by the Stockwell Crew in order to visit his girlfriend. The fact that Junior had nothing to do with any gang and was a sixteen-year-old boy studying hard for his GCSEs was irrelevant. He was seen, chased and beaten senseless by a group of Stockwell Crew members. He had got away with broken ribs, a broken jaw and a number of internal abdominal injuries. But he lived.

This "slight" required avenging. The fact that Junior was a stranger to the Kennington Homies was immaterial. Face had been lost. So a group of young men, all sixteen and seventeen had travelled by car to Stockwell, in full view of the CCTV cameras, and found and attacked two seventeen-year-old boys. They could be seen getting out of the car, blades, or to use the argot of the day, "shanks" in hand and simply set upon the two victims. Whether they knew who they were looking for, or whether it was chance, both young men attacked had numerous gang-related convictions, and could, therefore, be said to be members of the Stockwell Crew. It did not help them. One Delroy Prince was stabbed numerous times, including through the heart and died at the scene. His friend, Naseem Mbutu, also suffered multiple injuries, including having his liver almost cut in half, but through the genius of the paramedics and doctors lived, eventually making a full recovery. He was key prosecution witness number one. Not that his services were required. The CCTV was so comprehensive in that area, partly because this sort of thing was all too frequent, that the whole attack was caught on camera. Four lads got out of the car, leaving our client, Jimmy Consuelo, behind as the driver. When the attack was over there was a brief victory dance before they all piled back into the car and headed back to Kennington. All five had pleaded not guilty. Our defence was the unlikely, but just about tenable, "I did not know what they were going to do. Had I known, I would not have given them a lift." The others, were, it seemed, running self-defence. The trial was set down for five weeks. Were it to have taken place in the 1950s, it would have been unlikely to last five days. However, because of the age of the defendants, and the fact that one of them was being held at a special home in Kent, we did not start before 11am. With the breaks afforded to young defendants, one of whom had severe learning difficulties, the judge had agreed at the outset that we would knock off at 3.30pm. My task was to act as liaison between my leader, once again Humphrey Easter QC, who was not a big fan of going to the cells, and the client. In court I had to keep an accurate note and stay awake. Not, perhaps, the toughest of gigs.

It provided, though, a series of free advocacy lessons. At the Old Bailey there are a group of specialist prosecutors known as Treasury Counsel. Divided up into Senior Treasury Counsel, (who are QCs) and Junior Treasury Counsel, who are all ferociously bright and work extremely hard. They view themselves and are viewed by everyone else as the best of the best. That they come equipped with charm and a sense of humour as well, is simply unfair. On these facts an idiot would be odds-on to secure a conviction, but these things are not left to chance. With this being a multi-handed murder we were graced with a Senior TC leading a Junior TC.

Meanwhile the Defence QCs were all household names and all at the top of their game. Listening to them in court you could sit there and find yourself thinking that the moon is, in fact, made of cheese. Our jury were the usual London mixed bag in terms of age, gender and ethnicity. Unsurprisingly, given what was at stake, all took being a juror on this sort of case very seriously, witnessed by the volumes of notes being taken as the evidence unfolded. Watching the five defence silks deal with Naseem Mbutu was a privilege. Had that been the only prosecution evidence we'd have been home free. He was made to admit that he had started it, that he too had a shank, and having been allowed by the judge to refer to it, his background and membership of the Stockwell Crew was ventilated at length. One tiny problem though: the CCTV. It could not have been clearer if the BBC had turned up at the location with two days' notice and some floodlights. And it was damning, at least for the four lads who had got out of the car. This was just the sort of juicy newsworthy case that I had joined the criminal Bar to be a part of, however minor. It proved an effective tonic to my battered spirit.

What also helped was that spring was in the air and the motor racing season was due to start. At the end of week two of the trial was the first meeting that my car was eligible for, a ten lapper at Snetterton, so I had entered. Snetterton was another old wartime airfield circuit, this time twenty-odd miles south of Norwich. Shorter than it had been in the 1950s and 1960s it was taken over by Motor Sport Vision in 2004. They had lavished some much-needed cash on it and built a twisty infield extension. They had also erected some high banks from which spectators can view almost all the track. Technical and not particularly quick, it was not my favourite circuit, but hell, it was good to be back out. Humphrey gave me dispensation to scarper at lunchtime on the Friday so that I could get to my parents and the car in reasonable time. I loaded up and got to the B&B down the road from the circuit in time for a couple of beers and a bite to eat.

Saturday dawned with fog. Thick fog. The sort of fog that deadens sound. As a result, signing on and scrutineering appeared to be conducted by Trappists. We were due out as first practice at 9am sharp, but the rule is that you cannot race if one marshals' post cannot see or be seen by the next one on in the chain. Ten o'clock came and went. It was not until 10.45am that the sun made its presence felt and burned off enough of the mist. The organisers then had to squeeze three hours' practice into just over one and a half hours. This they did by truncating each session. If you were unfamiliar with the track: bad luck. You got an "out" lap, four quick laps and then an "in" lap. I had not raced there, although I had done a track day some years before the circuit had been altered. Some drivers were better than others at reading a new track. It was not the strongest part of my game. The competition was a mixed bag of fifties saloons, sixties saloons and some GT cars. Amongst that lot I was happy to be mid-grid at best. I was still improving when the chequered flag came out. I slowed immediately to allow as much cooling air through the radiator and motored slowly back to my berth.

There was just under an hour before we were due out, so I opened the bonnet for final checks. Oil level, OK. Water level, OK. Brake fluid level, OK. Checking the gearbox oil level and the diff level would require a jack which I did not have. Wing that. Perhaps the most important check was the mental state of the driver. That could best be described as full of clouds and incapable of going through the unpleasant, but essential, processing of adrenaline, yawns and all. Not, then, in the greatest shape to race a car at ten tenths. I did manage a few minutes quiet time before we were called into the assembly area.

The marshal blew his whistle and I tightened my belts, pulled on the balaclava, crash helmet and gloves, feeling hollow inside. We paraded down the pitlane and cruised round, forming up on the grid. Ahead was a Mark 2 Jaguar and an Anglia and next to me was an early sixties BMW. Time to concentrate. Select first gear at the five second board, 5000rpm on the clock, red lights on… Go! I dropped the clutch and had the rear wheels spinning perfectly. It was one of my better starts and by the time I was braking for the first corner, Riches, I had passed four cars. Good boy. I kept it tidy, swung through the corner and was gaining on the next group. Turn two, or Montreal as it is now known, was, when I was last here, a quickish right hander. Now it was a wide hairpin which turned back into the infield. No progress here. I had not really got to grips with the new layout and lost ground, being overtaken by one of my start line victims before we hit the back straight. At the end of that was a very quick left, but, as at Castle Combe, it could not be taken on its own merits because very shortly after it was a tight right hander. Not quite as punishing as Quarry, but it could cause problems if one arrived going too quickly. As we proceeded round the first lap I was surprised to see spots of rain on the windscreen. I had not spotted the clouds rolling in. The level of fear went up a notch, but with it the realisation that if I drove within myself some of my competitors might over reach themselves, or to use the phrase popular with Australian commentators, "chuck it at the scenery". At Coram, a seemingly endless right hander, oil had been dropped and instead of watching the others make a balls of it, I managed two full three-sixty degree spins. I got the car pointing the right way without losing a place, although the Anglia that I passed at the start was now welded to my back bumper. In theory a Lotus Cortina was a lighter more powerful car, but I couldn't shake him off. At the last left hander before the pit straight he posted one up the inside of me, such that the two of us arrived at the turning-in point on the same piece of road. Option one: turn into him and bugger the consequences. Option two: give way. Not being Lewis Hamilton and as I was paying for any paint swapping myself, I went for option two. He squeezed past, but on a sub-optimal line, so I had the faster car as we braked for Riches. With the positions reversed he was courteous too, and remained behind me through the twisty stuff. As we hit the back straight, I should have pulled away but his car was every bit as quick as mine and he simply slipstreamed past me into Brundle. So it went on for the rest of the race, passing each other more than once a lap, sliding through the corners, skittering about under braking and having a proper bunfight. The last corner was a carbon copy of the first lap, with him slipping by under braking, and he was still ahead at the flag. Good driving, and better fun.

Our grid had been selected for weight tests so we were herded into the scrutineering bay in a rough queue. As I slithered out of the car, having shed hat and gloves etc., I went over to the Anglia. "James Westerfeld," I said. "Well driven. I really enjoyed that."

"Stan Harrison," he replied, shaking my hand. "That is the first race I have done since 1968."

"Oh, right. What were you racing then?" I asked.

"Formula two," he said smiling.

"So you were a pro?"

"Not quite," he said "But I was up against the best. I beat Gerry Birrell once."

"Respect!" I said, impressed. "Why did you stop?"

"Lack of cash, a new wife and the strange demand that we have decent accommodation for a forthcoming child, rather than a camper van," he said.

"And what have you got under the bonnet of your car? That thing flies."

"I've been building race engines for other people for years. I thought that I would do one for me. I'm pleased with it. Goes all right," he smiled.

"Better than all right. I should have left you for dead in a straight line, but you stayed with me."

"We should do this again," he said, "are you doing all the races in this series?"

I could hardly tell him the truth. "Not sure of my commitments, but hopefully, yes."

"Good," he said and turned to push his car towards the scales.

I spent some of the rest of the afternoon watching the racing before loading up to return to reality. If this was the last time I did this, it had at least been fun. Nothing, but nothing, clears the mind of unwelcome rubbish better than racing cars.

24

Back in London, spirits definitely lifted, it was the start of the Defence case. Stabber number one was up to the plate first and spent a truncated day explaining that he had acted in self-defence throughout. He had had a shank with him because he had been threatened the night before by some bigger boys that he did not know. He kept it together, at least until he was cross examined. As is the custom the other Defence counsel went first, none of whom saw it in their interest to take his version apart. After lunch on day two of his evidence Garret O'Driscoll QC, leading for the Crown, stood up. For the first hour or so he was gentle enough, but without the change of wind being necessarily detectable, he gradually started to ramp up the pressure. Given that Naseem Mbutu had had his record put before the court, the Prosecution had applied for the jury to hear those of the first four defendants on the grounds of balance. The judge had agreed. They did not make happy reading, and quite a while was spent going through that. The next morning he really got stuck in, performing something of a textbook demolition of a lying witness. Courteous throughout, he never raised his voice once, and was all the deadlier for the charm. At the end of it, Defendant number one's case was in ruins. The others now knew what to expect.

Defendant number two, having watched his mate being turned inside out had a lengthy conference in the cells with both his counsel and his solicitor, and eventually emerged and said that he would not be giving evidence. When the judge asked whether he appreciated that this was his opportunity to give his account and that not doing so was capable of being held against him, the refusal had the jury's eyebrows vanishing into hairlines.

Defendant number three did go into the witness box and proceeded to give us a re-run of Defendant number one's performance. Not bad in chief (i.e., when answering questions from his own barrister), but it was downhill from there. O'Driscoll got him to admit stabbing Delroy Prince and intending to commit serious harm while he did so. In other words, he got him to admit murder. That Defence speech was going to be interesting!

Defendant number four broke cover but, while maintaining his denials throughout, looked like just the sort of chap who would stab a rival.

Then it was Jimmy's turn. In the days leading up to this moment I had been down in the cells with him as often as was allowed, time down there being rationed, asking him to pay close attention to how his compadrés got on, and repeatedly gave him my usual homily about *how* to give evidence: don't mumble and stare at your shoes, nice clear voice, look at the jury, don't argue with counsel, if you want a break ask for one, and so on. He said that he was ready. I was not convinced, but the moment was upon us. Of all of them, he was the only one with a glimmer of a chance. Humphrey took him through it slowly and carefully and I was surprised how good he sounded. I try not to look at the jury during a trial, but I sneaked the odd glance and those that were not making constant notes looked as if they were at least taking what he said seriously. Once again co-defending counsel had no urge to start a war they did not need, so the main threat remained Garret O'Driscoll. With our man there was no gentle start. We got the sixteen-inch guns from the start, and to my astonishment, Jimmy stood up to it: "Unlike the others, I have a job. I am the main breadwinner for my mother and brothers and sisters. I would not jeopardise all that for some gang war I am not a part of." His record was slender: shoplifting aged thirteen and allowing himself to be carried in a stolen car aged fifteen were hardly the stuff of the Kennington Homies, so we put that in. "Defendant two is a near neighbour whom I have known since school. He asked me to give them a lift so I said 'yes'. He promised that there and back would take no more than half an hour. Had I known what they were really up to I would not have gone near Stockwell. In any event, to do him this favour, we were there so long that it meant that I missed my weekly karate lesson, which I love." Garret could not disagree with that, as the prosecution had checked out the day of the week of, and attendance record at, karate, and what he had said was true.

People assume that what is said in court is key. And it is undoubtedly important. But as important is the *way* things are said. A furtive-looking witness is much less likely to have his account accepted than a matter-of-fact one. Best of all though, and when defending all too rare, is the faint air of bewilderment in a client that they became involved in the subject matter of the case and therefore, now find themselves in a Crown Court. We were in one of the Edwardian show courts, which is a pretty majestic room, and as Jimmy was grilled he occasionally looked about him as if to wonder: how the *fuck* did I end up in here? The overall impression he gave was much more positive than I had dared hope.

The Defence cases had taken a week, so speeches would follow on Monday. Humphrey and I spent an hour and a half late on Friday afternoon, in one of the many wine bars that surround the Old Bailey, sharing a bottle of Chablis and roughing out what he would say when it was our turn. We both agreed that our case was the only one that had improved as a result of going into the witness box. It was one of the oldest adages of the criminal Bar, that the highest point of the Defence case was at the conclusion of the Prosecution case. Most defendants cocked it up from there.

Come Monday, before we got to actual speeches, though, there was a lengthy discussion as to the law in the absence of the jury, with His Lordship indicating that this was just the sort of case that merited a split summing up. All parties agreed. So in just under an hour in the run-up to lunch (or "the short adjournment" as strictly it is still known) he took the jury through the law of murder and, very much with Jimmy in mind, the law of joint enterprise. What was in his contemplation? What was the position if they found as a fact that he was aware that all the others were carrying knives? What if he did not? And so on, a complicated legal area delivered with clarity and skill. So that the jury did not have to either write it all down or misremember what he said, he gave them written directions which they could take with them and refer to in retirement.

Speeches had always been my favourite part of the case, and with the talent on show I was really looking forward to hearing how each silk put their case. This not being some second-rate TV show, the prosecution went first. Garret started after the break and spent the rest of the day setting out why, in relation to each defendant, the proper verdict was one of murder. What he said was utterly compelling in relation to the first four defendants, helped by replaying sections of the CCTV. The next morning he came to Jimmy. He backed right off, leading me to wonder if he had been persuaded by his evidence. He took the jury through the law on joint enterprise in short order, pointing out that it beggared belief that he was not a fully briefed member of the team. It was in total contrast to his approach in cross examination. Beware the smiling assassin, though. He too was clearly an amateur psychologist, and must have taken the view that, in Jimmy's case, wearing hobnailed boots would be counter-productive.

Defendant number one was up next. Given the state of the evidence against his man it was a bravura performance. Trouble was, while the jury did not quite sit there with their arms folded, looking at their watches, one could see that they weren't buying from that stall. Defendant number two, who had not given evidence, at least was spared the need to apply the araldite to his evidence, but got much the same reception.

On Wednesday morning, I was really looking forward to how Howard Spencer QC would address them on behalf of Defendant number three. After his evidence, during which his client had admitted murder, he and his entourage had spent much time in the cells, presumably deciding whether the best approach from here was to throw their hand in. No, was the ultimate conclusion, but it made Howard's task almost impossible. He could hardly pretend that his client had not said what he had said. So, he gave them a history lesson about the need for independent juries and that in this very building, William Penn, later founder of the State of Pennsylvania had been on trial for unlawful assembly. The judge, unhappy with the jury's findings locked them up for two straight days. When they returned, they acquitted the defendants and were promptly fined for contempt of court and locked up again until they had paid the fine. The Chief Justice of The Court of Common Pleas ruled that the jury could not be punished on account of the verdict they returned. So, members of the jury, be independent. All good stuff and beautifully delivered, but as our judge, HHJ Standish QC, was visibly a beacon of fairness, there was not much to rail against. You could almost see the jury thinking: Bravo! But no cigar…

Defendant number four fared little better, not helping himself during his counsel's speech on his behalf, by starting a shouting match in the dock with one of the others.

Then Humphrey rose slowly to his feet and suddenly all twelve jurors looked alert with pens in hand. Much better. In just under an hour he painted much of the Crown's case as supposition and guesswork, with no assistance from the CCTV in relation to Jimmy. He asked them not to penalise a young man who was doing his best in difficult circumstances while living in a difficult area, for the actions of others. The speech started slowly but built and built, all delivered without apparent reference to any notes. I knew how much effort had gone into writing the speech, but I had not expected him to *learn* it. Best I could tell, though, that is exactly what he had done. It was a modern evocation of the sort of effort silks had once put in, in the days of capital murder. It was sublime and when he sat down there was the sort of silence which led one to suppose that the entire room had stopped breathing. So ended the business of the day.

On Thursday HHJ Standish summed up the evidence. Like all the best judges he knew better than to try and engineer a result, so he was scrupulously fair throughout. The jury retired just after lunch. The Bailey comes with a large Bar Mess/lounge on the top floor and we all retreated up there for a group chinwag. No doubt the prosecution team, as Treasury Counsel had a pile of work to do, but they came and chatted with us. The on-dit between us all was

Defendants one to four guilty of murder and an acquittal for Jimmy. Humphrey and I, though, thought that manslaughter for us was a distinct possibility, so held our optimism well in check. Everyone agreed that verdicts this week were unlikely. The rest of the day was spent pretending to catch up with paperwork and reading the newspapers.

Friday brought the same, but no verdicts.

On Monday morning the jury were sent out again at 10am on the dot. The Judge indicated that he would start thinking about giving the jury a majority direction towards lunchtime, if we had not heard from them. He would take any verdicts that were returned. We trooped upstairs, a cadre of barristers working, pretending to work, assailing their blood pressure with life-altering quantities of coffee and/or generally trying not to fret. Actually, it was worst for Humphrey and I. If you are defending an utterly hopeless case, this bit is easy. Justice is on its way. I did everything I could. Should there be a forensic miracle, well, aren't I marvellous? If you are defending someone with "a run", as it is known, it is torture. You cannot help running the whole thing through your mind in an imaginary tape loop. Have we done enough? What did I miss? They can't *possibly* convict on this evidence. Can they? And so on, ad nauseam.

Our jury must have been tuning in, for the tannoy went at noon: "All parties in Consuelo and others, please report to Court 2." This was it. I had seen Jimmy in the cells briefly mid-morning and he seemed quite calm. Once we were all assembled in court, though, he looked as if he was on the verge of throwing up. The Old Bailey is unusual, insofar as it is owned and run by the Corporation of London. The Lord Mayor of London is, notionally, the Lord Chief Justice, and can, thus attend court. Various aldermen or other City worthies often attend court, so when the usher brings the

Judge in, it is not unusual for him to be preceded by someone wearing their Dick Whittington Appreciation Society outfit, complete with, incongruously, a sword. Once we were all assembled, which took even longer here than normal, when the usher banged on the door and shouted "All rise!" three bods wearing eighteenth century outfits walked in with HHJ Standish bringing up the rear. I suppose it added to the drama. In short order verdicts were returned: Defendant number one guilty of murder, Defendant number two guilty of murder, Defendant number three guilty of murder and Defendant number four guilty of murder. He kicked off immediately and was dragged downstairs by the goalers, which only added to the pressure on Jimmy. For him alone, the jury had been given the option of an alternative verdict, to wit manslaughter. It took three or four minutes for other goalers to appear from downstairs and by then Jimmy was visibly shaking. The clerk of the court asked: "Madam Foreman, have you reached verdicts on Jimmy Consuelo upon which you are all agreed?" Answer: no. So they were directed that they could return verdicts upon him with which at least ten of them agreed. They were sent out again, while attention turned to when the others would be sentenced.

While the pressure on our client continued to mount, we had at least got them thinking. So we waited. And waited. The afternoon dragged on and we still had not heard from them at going home time.

The following morning I slipped into the cells for a quick chat with Jimmy. He looked pretty ashen, as well he might, but was able to grasp that at least in his case, there was everything to play for. It is, for obvious reasons, a little seen drama, but it is one of the most intense of any available today, anywhere.

It was just after lunch that the jury sent the Judge a note, and we were tannoyed to Court 2.

Once assembled, HHJ Standish unescorted today by overdressed rubberneckers, His Lordship told us that he had had a note from the jury that he could not disclose, but was minded to take any verdict that they might have. Did we all agree? Yes we did.

The clerk asked the Foreman to stand. "Madam Foreman, please answer my first question either yes or no. Have the jury reached verdicts upon which at least ten of you are agreed on either count?"

"Yes," said the Forman, "on count five."

"Members of the jury do you find Jimmy Consuelo guilty or not guilty of murder?"

An age passed… "Not guilty."

"Members of the jury have you reached verdicts upon which at least ten of you are agreed on count six?"

"No," said the Foreman.

"Thank you," said the Judge. He asked them whether, with the provision of more time, might they be able to reach a majority verdict on count six? They retired briefly behind the door to their retiring room and reappeared shortly afterwards, telling us that there was no prospect of a verdict on count six. They were promptly discharged from their service and left court with the Judge's warm words of thanks in their ears. Anyone who wanted to see the others sentenced should give their details to the court staff. The Crown had seven days to decide what they wanted to do about any retrial on the manslaughter. Then he rose.

So… not guilty of murder. The Crown had the right to go again. But they could not prosecute him for murder again, because they were obliged to respect the jury's verdict same as everyone else. It had been put on the basis that he had been in on it from the start, which, given the verdict was now untenable. Walking away from a case this serious was unlikely but it gave them a knotty legal and logical problem to solve if they wanted to prosecute him again.

We trooped down to the cells, Humphrey included, and had a surprisingly low-key chat with Jimmy. He had not really taken it in and was clearly emotionally spent. He would know his fate within a week. He just nodded.

25

So, what do you do when your heart is broken and you're about to be on trial on spectacular drug charges and you're unemployed and the only person you've spoken to in days is your bodyguard?

You go out with Flora Bascombe. That's what.

Of course, I couldn't go out by myself because that was what my life was like now apparently. But fortunately, Flora had a party to go to and a plus-one shaped gap that I could fill. With a little wheedling, she turned it into a plus-two; and so three weeks after getting back from Norfolk, Todd and I got suited and booted and headed off to the birthday party of a man we'd never met.

"Damn," Flora said, looking Todd up and down. "And you're who again?"

"Just a friend," Todd said. "Staying with James for a bit while my house is renovated."

"Well, I don't think anyone's going to mind you tagging along," she said.

"If you could stop ogling for five minutes, maybe we could head in?" I said.

Flora laughed. "Don't be jealous, James. We can't all look like action heroes."

I'd been surprised when Flora asked us to meet her at the foot of the Walkie Talkie building, and even more surprised when we were checked off a list and bundled into a lift.

We shot hundreds of feet in the air in seconds, and emerged into what seemed to be the tropics.

"Good, isn't it?" Flora said. "Bellsy always did know how to throw a party."

"Bellsy is the birthday boy?" I asked. We were handed glasses of champagne; Todd shook his head and took a flute of tonic water.

"No, silly, Bellsy is his wife," Flora said. "It's Fibby's birthday."

"Of course," I said. "Silly me."

Todd and I followed Flora into the fray. The vast hall was full of people, all dressed to kill; somewhere there was a string quartet, playing an improbably decent cover of Love Will Tear Us Apart. It was the last place anyone would think to look for me. It was perfect.

Not much of that evening has stuck in the mind. I drank four glasses of champagne very briskly, and almost physically felt the edges round off. It was a blur of bright colours, beautiful people, perfume, alcohol, the glitter of jewellery. I was at one point introduced to the host, Fibby, who turned out to be a red-faced investment banker named Phillip; his wife, Isabelle, had actually been a barrister in a previous life, and so we made cheerful, gossipy small talk. An enormous cake was wheeled out, alarmingly on fire. As parties went, it was a corker.

Somehow I ended up sitting on the stairs heading from one part of the garden to another, drinking very good cognac with a man named Bastien who owned a Bugatti Veyron; so, a prat, but an entertaining one.

"Max!" Bastien yelled. Someone turned around, and I was surprised to see that it was Max De Vries.

"Bastien," Max said, walking over. "And – hang on, *James*? What on earth are you doing here?"

"Friend of a friend," I said.

"Join us," Bastien said. "James was holding forth about – what was it, James? A corner called Malmaison?"

"Malmedy, I suspect," Max said. "James is a very good driver."

He sat down next to us, and Bastien offered him the cognac. For a while the three of us chatted happily about cars; even drunk, I noticed that Max was gently making fun of Bastien, which I couldn't help finding funny. When Bastien went to the loo, Max moved up a step to sit next to me.

"Heard you've had a bit of trouble," he said. "I'm surprised to see you out and about."

"Fiddling as Rome burns," I said. "Who knows when I'll be at a party again?"

"I'm sure it'll all blow over," Max said, and clapped my shoulder. "You're a good man, James."

To my horror, I found I was on the verge of tears. His unexpected kindness was more than I could entirely bear.

"Thank you," I said, thickly. "That's awfully good of you."

"Of course." Max got to his feet. "Now, I saw you arrived with Flora Bascombe. Shall we go and see where she's got to?"

Flora, it turned out, was dancing with Todd; a dozen couples were waltzing very loosely to what seemed to be a version of Kiss from a Rose. On spotting me, Todd grinned, and let me cut in.

For a little while, Flora and I danced in silence. She was dressed in something slinky, covered in little sequins; every curve glittered in the dim light. Her long hair had been pinned up, but a few loose dark curls had fallen artfully onto her cheek. Any man would have been lucky to be where I was right then.

"You're very quiet," Flora said.

"Just thinking," I said. "Are you having a good time?"

"Oh, yes," Flora said, smiling. "But then, I usually have a good time."

She meant it, too. Her life was so sunshiney; she seemed to live permanently in the first day of the summer holidays, happy and free and excited about the future. And all at once I was desperately sad. What I wouldn't give to be like that.

"I think I'm going to head home," I said.

26

The night before the trial, I slept. I had been anticipating staying up all night – had in fact laid in a decent single malt and the new Robert Harris – but instead I got into bed at eleven, turned over, and fell instantly to sleep. To be honest, I think I was beyond nerves. Nothing seemed real anymore.

It was bizarre, being in a court without the comforting armour of my wig and gown. Todd and I met Sara and David in the foyer, and seeing David in his, both of which were considerably cleaner and newer than mine, made me feel faintly sick.

"Chin up, darling," Sara said, spotting my expression. "You know today will be mostly faffing."

She wasn't wrong. The first bit of any trial was mostly faffing; organising bundles, swearing in the jury and waiting for the first witness who'd got caught in a traffic jam in Shepherd's Bush. It was so achingly familiar that for whole minutes at a time I could forget what was happening, and let myself drift into thinking that this was someone else's trial.

Eventually, we got going. Because I was a well-known London criminal practitioner, the powers that be had parachuted in Mr Justice Chance, who normally operated on the Northern Circuit. It was like most trials – an odd mixture of weirdly thrilling and mind-numbingly dull. Little of it sticks in my mind. I remember at one point David doing a very neat little bit of cross-examination about the reliability of a CCTV camera; I filed it away automatically, intending to steal it. His Lordship remained poker-faced throughout.

We broke for lunch. David had been joined by a pupil, a baby-faced blond boy, who went and got us all sandwiches from the Pret across the road. We'd managed to get a conference room to ourselves. Sara and David spent the hour working. Todd spent it reading a book called *Understanding Wine Technology: The Science of Wine Explained*. When his phone rang, he looked deeply unimpressed to have been interrupted.

"Stay here," he said to me.

"Yes, Dad," I said. He gave me the finger, and we both laughed. He disappeared into the corridor.

"Mr Westerfeld?" It was the pupil. He had been quietly making notes in a blue book until this point, but now he was looking at me.

"Hi," I said. "What can I do for you?"

"I was wondering – do you know a good barrister's accountant? David's is much too fancy for me, and I'm shit at maths."

I couldn't help it; I burst out laughing. The pupil grinned.

"It looks like mine is going to have a vacancy," I said. "Give me some paper and I'll give you her details."

I was halfway through writing the email address when Todd ducked his head around the door. His expression gave nothing away.

"James," he said. "I need you."

I smiled apologetically at the pupil, and joined Todd in the corridor.

"What is it?" I asked.

"That was my mate Keith," Todd said. "He's the one keeping an eye on Claire's place today. About ten minutes ago, a car he didn't recognise came screaming out of their driveway, headed north. He headed over immediately, and found the place in chaos – all the lads arguing, kids crying, a bucket of paint knocked over. Seems some bloke in fatigues rolled up, grabbed Claire, and legged it."

I felt the ice grip my stomach. "No," I said. "It can't – "

"Keith's called in some backup, but they'll be a while," Todd said. "So I'm going to head up there to help him."

"I'm coming too," I said. "Obviously."

"Mate." Todd looked me dead in the eyes. "I may have been to the law school of 'watching CSI on the telly', but I reckon the criminal legging it halfway through the trial is generally considered a bad idea."

He was right, of course. I looked back through the glass wall to the conference room, where Sara and David were talking quietly, heads bent together. They were working so hard for me; if I left that work would have been for nothing. And more than that: my life would be conclusively, unsalvageably finished.

"I don't care," I said. "It doesn't matter. It's Claire."

Todd nodded. "Thought you might say that," he said. "Come on – I've got a quiet way out of here."

We walked calmly down a service corridor and paused at a window which had clearly belonged to the original building; it was older than most of the surroundings, and looked out over an alleyway. Usually, this window was locked with a fiddly double wire padlock. Currently, it was open, letting in a smell of industrial chemicals and sweat. There was scaffolding all the way up this side of the building. The court's roof was being redone.

"You have to be kidding," I said.

"Shut up and do it," Todd said.

I climbed out of the window, out onto the shockingly precarious ledge of the scaffolding. He followed me out, then deftly picked my phone from my pocket and threw it back in through the window.

"Can't be too careful, mate," he said. "Come on, let's move."

We climbed carefully down the ladders, which in some places were attached very loosely. I have never been so glad to be back on solid ground. As soon as Todd's feet hit the ground he was off, jogging around the corner to where he'd parked the Sentinel. I followed, and the car was moving almost before I'd closed the passenger door.

If the previous drive to Norfolk had been tense, it was nothing on this one. We more or less obeyed the traffic rules inside London, but once we were out on the motorway Todd screamed along, clearly unconcerned about any consequences. I gripped the frame of the door next to me, and closed my eyes, and tried desperately not to think.

When we reached Thetford, Todd rang Keith.

"Location," Todd said.

"It's an old golf course." Keith's Somerset accent was so thick you could have spread it on toast. "Looks like no-one's been here in years. As far as I can tell, they're in the clubhouse. I'll text you the location – I'm waiting on the eastern perimeter."

"We'll be there soon." Todd hung up the phone, and the Sentinel lurched forwards even faster.

We pulled to a halt worthy of a rally driver in what looked to be a disused carpark, surrounded on three sides by trees. There was only one other car parked, a nondescript Land Rover that looked like it had last been cleaned in the Thatcher years. We got out and Todd immediately jogged over to a picnic bench half-hidden in the trees. It was occupied by a man who looked exactly like a children's book picture of a farmer: checked shirt, gilet, muddy walking boots, marks on his trousers where dogs had clearly jumped up. But his expression was hard.

"Update," Todd said.

"Perimeter scouted," Keith said. "Three cars on the property – two 4x4s, and an old Audi from the 90s. I've got a map." He pulled out an iPad. "Two main blocks of buildings – a clubhouse at one end, and what looks like a set of loos and a bar at the other. I'd make the clubhouse as the more likely location."

"Agreed," Todd said. "Two-man canoe?"

"That was my thinking," Keith said.

Todd nodded. "Alright," he said. "D'you have spare kit in the car?"

"Waiting for you in the boot," Keith said.

"Come on," Todd said.

What was waiting for us in the boot were, to my surprise, clothes – more checked shirts, patched jackets, and heavy boots. Todd stripped unselfconsciously, and so I did too, throwing my best suit into the Land Rover after Todd's polo shirt and chinos, and pulling on whatever he handed me. Within two minutes, we were Anonymous Farmer #2 and #3.

"You're not going to be in the action," Todd said. We'd piled into the Land Rover, which to my complete surprise ran like a hot knife through butter along the track. "I want you to be our lookout." He handed me an old-fashioned Nokia mobile from the mid-2000s. "Anyone shows up, you call us – it's speed-dial 1 – and start talking about haylage."

"Haylage?"

"It's a crop thing, don't worry about it. Just sound convincing. If anyone approaches you, you're a local farmer;

someone parked on your land, and you're looking to pick a fight about it."

"Haylage," I said again. "OK. I can do that."

"Good," Todd said. "This should be quick and easy. We park the car and jump out. You stick by the front entrance. We'll sweep the building, grab Claire, and get the fuck out of here."

"OK," I said again. The whole thing seemed even less real than the trial had. "Got it."

"Good, because we're here."

The Land Rover pulled up and we jumped out. The clubhouse was a squat concrete building, with picture windows on the far side and what looked like a staff area at the back. Todd and Keith nodded and disappeared into the building.

I took up what I hoped was a suitably casual position by the front door and waited. It was a clear, cool day, and from this vantage point you could see for miles: gently rolling lawns becoming greens becoming fields. There was no sign of any other people. Apart from the patches of golf course which had resisted the spread of weeds, it looked as though no-one had ever been there.

I counted off the minutes. It was agony, waiting; and yet there was nothing else I could do.

And then, around the corner of the clubhouse, I heard something. It sounded like the rasp of metal on metal, and it was coming from the back courtyard.

I knew I was supposed to stay put. I knew the smart choice was to call Todd and Keith. But what if it was nothing? I would just walk casually around the corner, just to check – I stopped in my tracks. There, kneeling on the ground, was a man in dark suit trousers and a pale shirt. He was sorting through a huge toolbox, piling the contents into two categories. The larger pile was heavy, dangerous-looking things; spanners, hammers, an enormous ratchet.

The man looked up, and shock slammed into me.

It was Timo Aristophanes.

27

The hammer-blow of comprehension exploded through my body. It had been Timo. It had all been Timo. Of course it had. He'd been one of Bill's clients; he'd known exactly how Bill could be manipulated. He had the money to bribe Bill, to buy the heroin, to have me kidnapped...to kidnap Claire in Antigua, when he thought she'd figured out the truth. Flora's friend had even mentioned a yacht. He had been at the races – he'd been inside the trucks. It was Timo.

"James," he said.

"You," I said. "It was you."

"No, it wasn't," Timo said. His voice was calm, but I noticed that he hadn't put down the oversized spanner he was holding. "James, take two seconds here."

"Where's Claire, you bastard?" I yelled.

"I don't know, and *shut the fuck up*," Timo said. "They'll hear us if you keep on like that."

"Who will?"

Timo looked at me with an expression of astonishing disdain. "The people who took Claire, you idiot," he said. "Now get over here and arm yourself."

"No," I said. "No – it was you. You got Bill to smuggle the drugs in the vans. You threatened him when he wanted to stop. You caused that crash at Goodwood."

"No I didn't," Timo said. "I didn't do any of those things."

"You lying – "

"James, I wasn't even *at* Goodwood."

Oh.

Oh, fuck, he hadn't been. I even remember talking to Terry about it before the race started – he was friends with a mechanic who'd worked with Timo a few years back. Timo had been at a wedding back in Greece.

"It wasn't you," I said.

"No, it wasn't," Timo said. "Now get over here and make yourself useful. I've sent my security over to the front, so I don't want to go in unarmed."

I walked over to him, and he handed me two of the spanners. "I reckon these will do something," he said. He still had the oversized spanner in one hand, and a hammer in the other. "Let's do this."

"My bodyguard – he and his partner have gone inside to scout…"

"So we'll go and look around the back," Timo said. "Time is of the essence."

And so we crept around the side of the building, tools in hand. I could feel every beat of my heart, hammering against my chest. Just when I was beginning to get used to it, we heard footsteps coming towards us.

"James you daft fucking Pom," Todd said. He and Keith emerged from a side door. "What the fuck are you doing?"

I considered trying to explain, and then considered that I was holding a spanner like a rounders bat while dressed like Farmer McGregor, and gave up.

"Alright, we've done a first pass," Keith said. "We reckon we've found the room. It's a big conference room on the second floor – no windows. There are two blokes built like brick shithouses guarding the only door."

"So now what?" Timo asked.

"Who the fuck are you?" Keith asked. "You know what, never mind – the plan's the same anyway. We wait for our backup, then mount an assault."

"We're just leaving Claire in there?" I asked.

"She's either dead already or they're not planning to kill her," Keith said. "Either way, she's not going anywhere fast."

"I have a security guard out here somewhere," Timo said. "Would five of us be enough?"

"Not when two of us are you two," Todd said. "No offence, mate, but neither of you are much use unless the problem is driving a rust bucket from the dawn of time around in a circle."

"What about…?"

But Timo never got to finish his sentence because he was cut off by the almighty crash of a body going through a window. All at once, it was chaos; we all ran around the building to find three enormous men wrestling each other on a bed of glass-strewn gravel. Todd, Keith and Timo went to break up the fray, but because I was slower than them I caught sight of the figure darting out of the building towards the Land Rover. Even at that speed, I would have recognised him anywhere.

It was Max De Vries.

"Timo!" I yelled. Timo looked up, and saw Max just as he reached the Land Rover.

"Oh, fuck," Timo said. "They left the keys in the car, didn't they?"

"Yes," I said.

"I'll…"

But once again he was cut off – this time, by a woman's scream from above.

"Claire," he said. His face was suddenly pale. "I have to – "

"Max is getting away, Timo!" I yelled.

Timo turned back to me, and tossed me something. I automatically reached out and caught it. It was a set of car keys.

"My Jag," he said. "It's just past the bank."

And then he was gone, bolting inside. I looked down at the car keys in my hand and then I realised that I needed to start running. I ran out past where we'd parked the car; ran up and over the slope enclosing it, and skidded down to almost crash into the side of a stunningly beautiful F-type Jaguar. I fumbled the door open, threw myself inside, and started the engine.

The Land Rover was just visible, hurtling down an access road at high speed. I tore after it, the Jag roaring into action; within seconds, I had a clear view of the Land Rover. For all that it looked like it was two cattle grids away from falling to pieces, that thing moved like stink – some tiny, wild part of my brain wondered what engine Keith had jammed into it. But even the best tuner in the world couldn't work miracles; I was gaining on him, and fast.

We were rocketing along a narrow access road, barely more than a single lane. We took a sharp right turn, tyres screaming, and hit an even narrower road, lined on both sides by enormous oak trees, their branches bent so deeply that the road had in essence become a tunnel, dark and claustrophobic. I grew closer to the Land Rover, then closer still, until I was right behind it. My plan had been to overtake, then skid to a halt, forcing the Land Rover to stop.

But instead, Max spun the wheel to the left, and crashed directly into the trunk of a tree.

By the time I got out of the Jag, the Land Rover was already on fire.

At once, I was back at Goodwood once more, watching Bill Akely's car smash into the bank, but this time I could smell the burning fuel and rubber and hot metal, and the same horrifying crackle of things bending and snapping under pressure.

For a long moment, I just watched. My body froze; all I could do was follow the flames as they rose higher and higher. And then I saw that inside the car, Max was still moving.

I would like to say that no part of me hesitated, but that would be a lie. For one long second, I considered just letting him burn. He deserved it, over and over.

I ran over and began to pull him from the burning wreckage.

I will never forget those few minutes before Todd and Keith showed up. I managed to wrestle the door open; even with my shirt sleeve wrapped around my hand, the metal was searingly hot. As the door swung open I was hit in the face by a wall of heat and the stink of burning fuel. Max was slumped forwards over the steering wheel, blood cascading from a cut on his forehead, more blood spreading slowly up his arm, which looked to be horrifically broken. He had not been wearing his seatbelt, so I got my arms under his shoulders and began to drag him out of the car. He was a deadweight, barely conscious, moaning in agony; up close I could see that his face was one vast livid burn. I felt something burning on my own skin, on my neck, my cheek, my hands, but I couldn't stop. I just kept moving backwards, dragging Max's legs out of the footwell, his body clear of the wreckage, until we were both safely on the other side of the road. I collapsed next to him, every inch of me filthy and exhausted, pain exploding along my left arm. I wanted to get back into the Jag, to drive us both back to the clubhouse, to find Claire, Todd Keith and Timo, but I couldn't move. All my energy was spent. All I could do was wait.

And so I sat there on the side of the road next to Max De Vries, and closed my eyes, and waited for the cavalry to arrive.

Epilogue

It was a beautiful June day, and I was about to go racing.

"Sure you're ready for this?" Michael asked, for the thousandth time. We were suiting up, although it would still be a while before we got out there.

"Yes," I said. "I am very, very sure."

"If your arm starts to – "

"Michael Ferguson, if you say one more thing about my arm I will bash you over the head with the nearest spanner."

Michael looked over at me, and grinned. "Alright," he said. "Guess you must be ready."

And I was. It had been more than two months since I'd been released from hospital; all that was left of my burns were scars, which the doctors had said would heal slowly. The worst of them was on my arm, where it turned out hot metal had seared straight through the sleeve of my shirt – I'd been so caught up trying to drag Max away I hadn't even noticed it. There were smaller scars on my face and hands, and a bigger one on my neck. But I was OK.

That was more than could be said for Max De Vries. I'd been unable to resist going to have a look at him the night before I left the hospital. Two special policemen were guarding his door, but when they saw it was me they let me through. He was asleep, knocked out by morphine; his injuries had been much more severe than mine. But the main thing that lightened my heart was the pair of handcuffs which kept him securely attached to the hospital bed. Max De Vries wasn't going anywhere fast.

In the end, it had been one of his employees who'd turned on him. Todd, Keith and Timo's security guard had collectively made mincemeat of the pair who had been guarding the conference room door, as well as the third man that Timo's security guard had thrown through a window. It was the one who'd gone through the window who caved. The final nail in his coffin had been found in Bill's holdall, of all things. Claire had handed it over to the police in charge of the investigation into Max, and they'd found his fingerprints on a bottle of Bill's eye drops which had been heavily doctored with atropine. Taken in sufficient dosage, atropine will stop the heart. Bill had been unconscious when he hit the bank. At the inquest the jury had returned a verdict of unlawful killing, so as well as the drugs enquiry, Max was facing a murder charge. The same jury had cleared the Goodwood authorities of any safety failings.

The press had gone insane. However many times we all declined to be interviewed, the stories kept coming, as wave after wave of details were uncovered. The most excruciating headline was in the *Telegraph*: "Hero Barrister Uncovers International Drug Ring". My mum had it framed and put up in the downstairs loo. I'd had the mother of all bollockings from a series of judges regarding my little stunt legging it from the trial, including an interview without coffee with the Lord Chief Justice. The CPS took a bit of persuading to drop all charges, but the fact that scarpering as I had, led directly to the case against me unravelling might also have had something to do with it. They had wanted to pursue a charge of absconding during the trial but I was told that Mr Justice Chance had "suggested" that such a course would be, in these circumstances, inappropriate. By the time I had left hospital, they had backed down. The Bar Standards Board were less forgiving, but I was led to believe that someone near the top had had a word. Those proceedings eventually melted away too.

"I'm going to grab some water," Michael said. "Get you anything?"

"Nah, I'm fine," I said. I sat down on a bench, miraculously free of tools, rags and other detritus, and closed my eyes.

"Do you mind if I join you?"

It was Timo.

"Of course not," I said. I moved over to let him sit down. Like me, he was suited up for the race.

"This heat is ridiculous," he said. "I thought English summers were supposed to be all rain."

"English summers do what they want," I said. "How are you doing?"

"Oh, very well, very well," Timo said. "Got my eyes on a beautiful little Ferrari for next season."

"Can't wait to see that," I said. "Tolly's going to lose his head completely."

"I'm sure," Timo said, smiling.

We sat in silence for a little while just listening to the soothing, familiar noises of pre-race preparation. I was so glad to be back.

"Timo," I said.

"James," he said.

"I wanted to ask you this, but you left before I got out of hospital," I said, "and no-one else would tell me anything. What were you doing out there, that day? How did you know something was happening?"

Timo smiled, and then turned to look straight ahead. I did likewise, watching, as he did, the satisfying click of a mechanic's spanner across the room.

"Once upon a time, I was at Goodwood," he said. "It was a beautiful evening the night before the race; the night of the Ball. I'd just fired my preparation team – one of them had been stealing from me – and I'd been told to talk to a man named Bill Akely. A friend introduced us, and we got along well. It was hard not to like Bill; he was such a happy person, so very kind-hearted. And then, just as we were getting down to the details, Bill was joined by the most beautiful woman I'd ever met."

Timo closed his eyes.

"I suppose there was nothing so unusual about her. She was very, very pale – too pale for most people's tastes – and a little older than most classical beauties. But from the moment she smiled at me, I was lost.

"Of course, there was nothing to be done. Bill and Claire were very happy together – their business was booming, their children thriving. Everything was good for them; a golden couple. And I didn't mind. Honestly, if I'd thought that she was the sort of woman who would leave her family in the lurch for a washed-up old playboy like me, I might have loved her less.

"When I heard that Bill had died – oh, I was distraught. I would miss Bill terribly; he was a good friend, but what had so upset me was the leap in my heart when I realised that Claire would be free. How could I be happy to think of her like this? I was so ashamed of my feelings that I didn't offer to help her, in the aftermath, something I sorely regret."

He shook his head. "And then she met you, and I knew any hope I'd had was lost. I hated you for a little bit, there. That first night in Portugal, it was so obvious what was going to happen, and I hated you for it. But when we found out you were missing, I knew what I had to do for her."

"It was you," I said. "You hired Mustapha."

"It was me," Timo said. "Yes. Mustapha and I met some years ago in…less than ideal circumstances, and he solved that problem so quickly and quietly that I knew he was the person to call."

"So all this time – Todd, and Doug, and Keith, and that doctor in Antigua…"

"It's been quite an expensive hobby, looking after you two," Timo said, and I could hear the smile in his voice. "My accountants are very pleased that it's come to a close."

"You did all this for us – for me – for Claire – "

"For Claire," Timo said. "Yes."

I finally turned to look at him. His expression was gentle. He was smiling.

"One of the things I loved about her was that she was so fierce," Timo said. "It wasn't right there at the surface, but you could sense it; I could, at least. She would do anything to protect her family. I loved that strength."

I knew what he meant. I thought of all the choices Claire had made since she'd gone to look for that lost earring and found her husband's secret. There was nothing she wouldn't have done to keep her family safe.

Timo stood up. "Best of luck out there, James," he said, and offered me his hand. I shook it. "You deserve a win."

"In a Lotus Cortina?" I said. He grinned. "And pigs will fly."

"Stranger things have happened, Mr Westerfeld," Timo said, walking away. "Have happened to you, even."

Michael came back, and we sat in companionable silence together for a while. We'd be heading back to Antigua later in the year for an actual holiday; we were already planning the bar crawl.

Suddenly, I needed a breath of air.

"Back in a second," I said. I ducked out into the shade of the courtyard of the Drivers' Suite, and rested my head against the wall.

"James."

I looked over. It was Claire. She was wearing a pale pink summer dress and a shawl, and looked almost rosy in the sunshine.

I grinned at her. "What are you doing here?" I asked. "You know you're not supposed to be back here."

Claire grinned back. "Well, no-one noticed me," she said. "Are you going to report me, Mr Westerfeld?"

I put my head to one side, considering. "I don't think I saw you," I said. "Definitely not. You can't possibly have been here, so you must not have been."

"Very good point." She was close, now, barely three steps away. "None of this can possibly be happening."

I closed the gap between us. She kissed me, and then looked up, smiling.

"Glad I'm here today," she said.

"Glad you're here, too," I said.

"Glad you gave me a second chance," she said, quietly.

I tilted her face up with one finger so we were looking straight at each other. "Everything you did had a reason," I said. "I would like to be one of the people you protect so fiercely."

"You are," Claire said. She kissed me again. "You will be."

The tannoy blared out from the hangar, calling all racers to the assembly area.

"I have to go," I said.

"You have to go," she said. "Best of luck, James."

She stood on tiptoes to kiss my cheek. I turned to head back inside; turned once more to see her, smiling, hair on fire in the sunshine.

Inside, Michael was waiting for me. "Come on, James," he said. "Let's see if we can give Timo a run for his money."

I grinned. "Stranger things have happened," I said and then put on my helmet, and headed out into the afternoon to go motor racing.

About the Author

Carruthers J. Lardy is a practising criminal barrister, formerly living in west London and now in East Anglia. He is a now-retired racing driver, a devoted fan of classic cars in general and historic motor racing in particular. Happily he is not as accident prone as our hero.

Milton Keynes UK
Ingram Content Group UK Ltd.
UKHW011322061123
432065UK00001B/33